PRAISE FOR HANNAH JAYNE

"What a ride! Full of twists and turns—including an ending you won't see coming!"

—April Henry, *New York Times* bestselling author of *The Girl Who Was Supposed to Die* on *Truly, Madly, Deadly*

"Teens who enjoy R. L. Stine and Christopher Pike are the likely audience for this gripping mystery."

—*School Library Journal* on *Truly, Madly, Deadly*

"This suspenseful thriller is well paced with carefully developed characters and sharp dialogue."

—*School Library Journal* on *See Jane Run*

"Well-rounded characters spark with life in this chiller."

—*Booklist* on *The Dare*

"Brynna's guilt-induced psychosis makes for a page-turner in the spirit of Lois Duncan's classic *I Know What You Did Last Summer*; it will undoubtedly please the thriller-loving crowd."

—*Kirkus Reviews* on *The Dare*

"This mystery is marked by gripping psychological suspense, and the plot builds to a dramatic conclusion."

—*Booklist* on *The Escape*

ALSO BY HANNAH JAYNE

Truly, Madly, Deeply
See Jane Run
The Dare
The Escape
Twisted

THE REVENGE

HANNAH JAYNE

sourcebooks
fire

Copyright © 2017 by Hannah Jayne
Cover and internal design © 2017 by Sourcebooks, Inc.
Cover design by Elsie Lyons
Cover image © Paul Knight/Trevillion Images

Sourcebooks and the colophon are registered trademarks of Sourcebooks, Inc.

Published by Sourcebooks Fire, an imprint of Sourcebooks, Inc.
P.O. Box 4410, Naperville, Illinois 60567-4410
(630) 961-3900
Fax: (630) 961-2168
www.sourcebooks.com

Library of Congress Cataloging-in-Publication data is on file with the publisher.

Printed and bound in the United States of America.
VP 10 9 8 7 6 5 4 3 2 1

To Lynlee Jayne, who was with me throughout this whole experience.

ONE

Tony

Hope reached out to me, the tips of her fingers brushing over my forearms, sending a barrage of goose bumps up my body. She was leaning in to me, close enough that I could see the light bounce off her glossy, pushed-out lower lip, could smell the faint scent of strawberry on her hair. Hope was the most beautiful girl in the world and she was mine, close enough to touch, to hold, to kiss, so close that I—

"Our love is a flower," she cooed.

The words pricked at the backs of my ears. Something wasn't right.

"Hope—"

The room wasn't as dark as I'd thought it was. The light shifted slowly, and I could make out shadows, rapt, staring. We weren't alone.

"That blooms…" Hope went on.

"No."

I could feel the burn up the back of my neck. Could feel sweat start to bead at my hairline.

"Hope, please don't." My voice sounded weird and high and pathetic. Hope's eyes flashed with something like an apology and then hardened into slits of silver. The edges of her lips turned up into the smirk I had once found so sexy but now cut at me and turned my stomach.

"That brightens each and every room…"

Her words dissolved into laughter that came from every corner, reverberating, thundering through my skull. The lights were on. I was in the school hallway, and everyone was pointing, laughing. Except for Hope. She was in the middle of them all, her serpentine tongue dashing across those stupid, glossy lips as she read my poem out loud. One eye quirked in a silent, biting threat. *Everyone's on my side, Tony.* She didn't even move her lips. *I brought you up from loser status just to crush you back down again.*

I woke up tangled in the sheets, my chest damp, my heart clanging like a fire bell.

Hope.

I kicked my legs over the side of the bed and dropped my head into my hands. "Jesus."

It had been just over twelve hours since I broke up with Hope Jensen.

I dumped the most popular girl in school.

I hadn't meant to, hadn't planned it. I really did love Hope. She was funny and smart and gorgeous—but she also had a mean streak that was hard to stomach. She was a pseudoceleb and a trust fund baby, so for the first few months when she made comments, I could brush them off. She didn't realize she was being shallow when she made the occasional snide comment about someone's clothes or hair or car. She didn't understand that not everyone lived the way that she did, that not everything was going to go her way.

We were different, and pretty soon the novelty of dating me, a poor kid so far out of her league, was going to wear off. I thought I was doing her a favor. I took her to the beach. Did it in private. Even made it look like it was all my fault. I thought we were cool. Hope agreed, we hugged, she said we would still be friends. The next day, she gave me a big, dazzling Hope Jensen smile and told everyone I had a raging case of herpes.

A day after that, Hope ripped my heart out in front of the whole school, then did a little tap dance on it by reading the letters I had written her out loud.

I wanted to forget about it, to forget about her, but after dating her for seven months, she was everywhere. Her cheerleading picture stuck to the side of my computer monitor. The homecoming court picture where one of her gorgeous, tanned legs jutted out of the slit of her dress. The selfies she called *usies*, our faces smashed together and taking up the entire frame.

I snatched one of those down and ripped it apart, tearing Hope in half right between the eyes.

My phone was glowing on the bedside table and I thumbed it, rolling down a line of tweets calling me everything from a loser to a wannabe to a pathetic loser wannabe.

Fucking Hope.

When I opened my laptop, she was there too—a collage of pictures of her grinning, strutting, posing, and making kissy faces while the students in the background adored her on my screen saver—just like I had. But that was over now. If she was going to mess up my life, I was going to mess up hers.

My fingers raced over the keyboard.

I went to every website I could think of. I signed Hope up for everything from breast pads to dating websites. I sent her free samples by the truckload—hemorrhoid creams, Depends, strawberry-flavored lube. Pet food samples. Hookup sites. Neo-Nazi support groups. Desert Storm survivor chat rooms. Hope Jensen, DOB: 5–19–00. Dial-A-Bride. Hot Singles in Your Area. Hope Jensen, blond hair, blue eyes. Tinder. LoveSpace. Bangbook. Hope Jensen, five foot seven, 108 pounds, "open to anything."

The sun was starting to break through the blackness outside and I yawned, glancing back at my glowing laptop screen. Hope's information was still up on my screen—phone number, email address, home address. Right before I logged off, a dialogue box popped up with a single question: *Share Location?*

My eyes flitted over the pictures of Hope surrounding my screen, the smile that now seemed smug, the eyes that suddenly seemed so hard and cold. I heard her voice in my head, that saccharine-sweet tone slipping over the words I had given to her, that I had given to her in confidence, in *private*.

I hovered over the share location question and clicked *Yes*.

TWO

I grinned when I drove past Hope's house the next morning. There was a pizza guy on the front stoop—gotta love those twenty-four-hour delivery guys—holding a half-dozen pies and jamming his finger against the bell. I could imagine Hope stomping through the mammoth front hall, her hair half-done, livid that someone would dare interrupt her beauty routine.

In chemistry, Hope made a big show of not sitting near me, telling Mr. Howard that she'd *prefer* a new lab partner while cutting her eyes to me, then rolling them dramatically.

Mr. Howard shrugged. "You can sit wherever you like as long as you turn your phone off."

Hope glared at her phone. "I can't help it. I'm getting, like, fifty calls every minute. I don't know how all these idiots suddenly got my phone number."

I had a hard time hiding my satisfied smile.

Angela, the girl who sat behind me and who would probably

end up being my new lab partner, kicked the back of my chair. When I turned around, she jutted her chin toward Hope and then raised her eyebrows.

Angela and I weren't really friends, just two kids who went to the same school. She was new last year and hadn't really joined any group that I knew of, but we were on pretty good terms. I leaned against her desk and lowered my voice to a whisper.

"It's possible I may have accidentally leaked a teensy"—I held my thumb and forefinger a millimeter apart—"bit of Hope's personal information. Like her phone number."

Angela's lips turned up into an appreciative half smile.

"And her address."

No one else was talking to me—unless you counted the guys who were my friends yesterday coughing *pussy* and *loser* into their hands every time I passed—so it felt good to have someone make direct eye contact.

"I'm surprised you even dated her," she whispered to me.

I shrugged, smiling to hide the sting. No one thought Hope should be with me. She was a knockout with a mean streak, and I was just…me. But for all her issues, she was awesome too. She had a tough exterior. She had to, she told me, because everyone always wanted something from her. But with me, she was soft. Or at least that's what I'd thought.

When the bell rang, Hope tossed me a last slicing glare before her two best friends flanked her and walked her out of the class-room, holding on to her arms like she would crumble from the stress of forty-two pizzas at any minute.

Angela came up alongside me, crossing her arms in front of her chest. "That girl's a real piece of work."

I nodded but kept my eyes on Hope. She let out a whoosh of air as her phone rang, then held it to her ear. Angela was saying something, but I was straining to hear Hope over the din. Then, loud, from Hope: "No, I am not up for whatever! That's disgusting! How did you get this number?" She let out one of her signature groans and stomped her foot.

Payback's a bitch.

The school day flew by, and Hope's name was on everyone's lips. They weren't talking about me, about our breakup; it was all Hope: *Did you hear that someone delivered forty pizzas to her house? Someone left a gross note on her car! Her phone has been blowing up.* I hung back, listening, laughing. There was a part of me that felt sorry for her, but that part was tiny.

Hope had ruined me for no reason. She had turned the school against me, and I didn't even know why. She was my *girlfriend*. She had told me she loved me, let me put my hand under that huge slit in her homecoming dress. I had loved her. I thought we could end on good terms. But clearly Hope didn't think that way.

She deserved everything that was coming to her.

THREE

My phone was ringing. I rolled over and knocked half the stuff off my nightstand before finding it.

"'Lo?"

"Tony?"

I sat up, rubbing my eyes and yawning. "Hope? What time is it?"

"It's nine thirty at night, you jackass. Were you asleep already?"

I glanced at the bedside clock and then at myself, lying on top of my sheets and fully clothed.

"No."

Hope sucked in a long breath and then dropped her voice. "Look, Tony. I know it was you. I know you put my name and address and phone number all over the Internet."

I wanted to feel proud of myself, but I was still confused and sleep-addled, somehow hoping that Hope was calling to apologize for spreading the rumor, for reading my poems out loud.

"You have to take it off."

"What?"

"My name. My picture. My info. You have to take it off the Internet, Tony. Right now."

The shrill tone of her voice cut through my fog and right down to my anger. "Why would I do that?"

"It's not fair."

"Like you humiliating me in front of the entire school?"

"You dumped me, remember?" Her voice was a tight snarl.

I was too angry to reconsider, to be taken aback. "And reading my letters out loud to your fan base? What the hell, Hope? What did I do to you? I thought we were good." I could feel the lump forming in my throat, and I tried to get angry again but couldn't. "You told me you loved me."

Hope paused for a beat. Her voice was soft. "Please, Tony."

"Please what?"

"Take my information off the Internet."

I was rubbing my temples, shaking my head. "You deserve whatever you get, Hope."

"Please!" Her voice was shrill but this time with a soft, quavering edge. "People have been calling me."

That made me smile. "And dropping shit off on your porch. I don't care. Just like you apparently didn't care about my feelings before you—"

"I think someone followed me home." There was a hint of desperation in her voice, but Hope could turn her emotions at the snap of a finger. She was an expert at getting what she wanted, going from cheerful and bubbly one moment to a sobbing, heart-wrenching mess the next. She was good.

"I'm sure it's probably one of your many admirers. Good night."

"No, please. Please, take everything down. I'm sorry, okay? I'm sorry and I think someone has been following me and I'm really scared. What if some psycho got my address off the Internet and is stalking me?"

I rolled my eyes. "Good-bye, Hope."

"Tony!"

It sounded like Hope had dropped the phone, probably kicking it for dramatic effect. Then I heard it: a scuffle.

The low grumble of a male voice.

A sharp *no* from Hope.

Arguing.

A faint scream. The *eek* of wheels peeling out. And then nothing.

FOUR

My pulse ratcheted up, and I pressed the phone to my ear, trying to hear more. I screamed Hope's name, but there was no response, no giggle followed by some insult so typically Hope—lame ass or dumb freak or jackwad. There was just silence.

"Hope?" Pause. "Hope, come on."

Silence.

I jumped out of bed and grabbed my keys and was halfway out the door before I figured it out: typical Hope.

Nothing was ever her fault. Things always went her way. Hope always got what she wanted. She was a pseudoceleb not just at school, but in town too. Her parents cohosted a morning news show, and Hope was their golden child: smart, pretty, sunshine-out-her-ass perfect. I had seen her work the system. She never paid for coffee or breakfast or anything at Effie's because the television was always tuned to Channel 7, and every morning Bruce and Becky Jensen smiled out at Effie's clientele and included the syrup-stained masses in their affable family banter. Thus, the prodigal daughter should never want for a scone or a lumberjack scramble.

She got out of speeding tickets and parking tickets and once nicked a car but got off with a warning because the other driver was "such a big fan."

Hope pretended that she hated dealing with the great unwashed—that's what she called everyone who fawned over her and her parents—but she reveled in it, even had a shelf in her room stuffed with plush animals and ugly trinkets that her parents' fans had given her. She also had a closet shelf loaded with booze and pills, uppers and downers courtesy of the other rich kids.

She had probably staged the whole scream-and-squeal. I imagined her screaming into the phone, then holding the thing up to her laptop as a car peeled out on *Furious 7*. She was probably laughing while my heart thudded against my chest as I looked for my keys, ready to save the day.

I sat back, stretched out on my bed again, and stared at my phone. Hope would call back any minute, furious that I hadn't dialed her a thousand times. She was probably counting the minutes now, waiting.

Any minute now.

She thought she knew me so well.

I glanced at the clock, watched the red glowing numbers on my alarm tick off minute after minute.

Damn it, Hope.

FIVE

"Going out, honey?"

My parents were snuggled on the couch, watching some old movie on TV. I flipped my keys, grateful that my parents were pretty hands-off, that between working since I was fifteen and basically striking out with girls until Hope came along I had earned their respect, their stamp of *He's too boring to worry about curfews.*

"Just going to run a quick errand."

My dad glanced at his watch. "It's after nine thirty."

"I just need to grab something for a project. Thirty minutes, tops. I'll be right back."

I was out the door before they could say anything else.

I dialed Hope three times in the twelve minutes it took me to drive to her place. I wasn't surprised when she didn't answer, just annoyed. Part of me knew I was playing right into her hands and hated myself for it. The other part was a tight ball of anxiety.

What if something actually happened to her?

I heard the scream in my mind again, the squeal of tires.

It sounded real—didn't it?

"She's messing with you," I told myself, gritting my teeth and biting down hard until my jaws ached. "She's just going to laugh when you get there…"

Hope's house—a massive estate set back from the private drive—was lit with outdoor lights, but the house itself was dark. I parked anyway and strode to the door, knocking.

"Hope!" I yelled. "It's me! Open up."

Nothing.

I glanced at my phone again, texted her, told her I was waiting outside.

No response.

I dialed her again, groaning, then cocked my head, listening to the stereo ringing going on: one on my phone, one on hers. Faint, but I'd recognize the ring anywhere—Hope had specialized rings for everyone. I pulled my phone from my ear.

"Hope?"

My phone kept ringing; so did hers.

I followed the sound down her porch, around the winding patch of golf-course-short grass. "Hope?"

The phone stopped ringing and went to her voice mail. I hung up, speed-dialed her again, and made a beeline down the walk, down the drive, then hunched into the gutter where the tune was slightly less muffled.

I poked at the mess of leaves caught in the gutter grate, my heart doing a double thump when a faded light flashed behind the debris. I pushed the leaves aside, and my own face was staring up at me as the phone vibrated and rang. The words *Call from Tony*

G. were warped by the dirt, by the broken glass on the face of the phone, but it was definitely Hope's phone. And it was in the gutter.

My heart started to pound. *Had she... Had it really...* I took a deep breath. Hope would pull out all the stops to make it look like she'd been kidnapped.

But her phone...

Hope's phone was her lifeline. She was never without it. I couldn't imagine her dumping it, even for a prank of this magnitude.

I picked her phone out of the gutter, shook off some leaves, smoothed off the dirt, and checked her call log. Her call to me. My return calls to her. Three calls from someone with the initials RR. Two calls back.

RR?

Renee Wright: ReRe, Hope's best friend. RR.

Cracked screen, cement-scratched edges. The phone had definitely been dropped—*or tossed*, I reminded myself.

I was still hunched over the gutter when the headlights cut through the night, flooded me, and burned my eyes. I glanced up, squinted.

"Everything okay here, son?"

It was the security guard who patrolled Hope's neighborhood. The guy was a rent-a-cop on a power trip who had caught me and Hope in her car or mine more times than I cared to count. We were both pretty sure he was a semicloseted perv who was into Hope and lived every day hoping he would catch her with her shirt off, but it was never going to happen. Hope liked the attention and trilled and drawled when he flooded our car with light, playing up her smeared lipstick and ruffled hair and acting all hot and bothered.

She liked to see his eyes go round and glassy, liked to see the flush in his cheeks, but the guy gave me the creeps.

He peered at me from his car now, eyes narrowed. As usual, all I could see were those beady eyes from under his Atlas Security hat, his lips pressed together as he scrutinized me. I pocketed Hope's phone and stood up, brushing my hands on my pants. "Yeah, just dropped my phone."

The rent-a-cop and I stared at each other for a beat. He seemed to be daring me to make the first move. Finally, "You visiting the Jensens tonight?"

I glanced over my shoulder as if checking that the house was still there. "Uh, no, no one's home. Just heading out actually."

The cop got out of his car, slamming the door behind him and walking slowly toward me. He had his hands on his hips, television cop–style, but instead of a gun belt, all he had was an enormous flashlight that hung halfway to his knee.

"So…" I thumbed over my shoulder toward where I was parked. "I guess I'm just going to go." I turned on my heel.

He kept his eye on me until I got into my car, then kept staring until I turned over the engine and backed into the street. I could see his headlights still fixed on Hope's driveway as I slowly drove away.

I got to school just before the first bell and strolled the halls, telling myself I wasn't looking for Hope.

I didn't want to, but part of me was genuinely curious. The other part was sure she was keeping to the dark corners so she could spring out at lunchtime and call me a dick for almost getting her kidnapped. Just like the rest of her life, it was probably some publicity stunt, another show for the whole school to laugh at me and fawn over her. For a girl who hated her parents with a fiery vengeance, she was just like them.

I filed into ethics with everyone else. Renee and Ashleigh—two of Hope's current BFFs—stared at their phones until the second the bell rang, then looked around, their overly made-up eyes falling on Hope's empty seat.

"Where's Hope?" Renee mouthed to me.

I rolled my eyes and shrugged, not wanting to play a role in another of their stupid games.

"Okay, okay, everyone, settle down." Mrs. Patten was always late to class, always carrying an armful of notebooks and a coffee mug she never seemed to drink out of. Renee's arm shot up.

"Yes, Ms. Wright?"

"Mrs. Patten, Hope isn't here today. Is it okay if I call her and check in?" Renee pointed to her phone as if to prove that her intentions were honorable.

Mrs. Patten blew out a sigh and shook her head. "No, Renee. If you want to call someone, please do it between classes."

"But Mrs. Patten, Hope didn't tell me she wasn't going to be here today. She tells me everything. I'm worried."

Mrs. Patten pinched the bridge of her nose like Renee was giving her a headache, which I'm sure she was. "She's probably just sick. Call her on your break."

I shifted in my seat, glad Mrs. Patten was strict. Hope's phone was rolling around in my glove box.

Renee's hand shot up again. "But Mrs.—"

"Not now!" Mrs. Patten snapped.

Class passed uneventfully, and when it ended, Renee was on her phone before the bell stopped ringing. I could see her face fall a little more with each ring, and my heartbeat started to speed up.

She's just trying to screw with you, Tony, I told myself. *Hope is fine, probably just hanging out at her house, eating bonbons and watching herself on old episodes of her parents' show,* Wake Up the Bay!

Hope's parents were never around, and she was a fan of taking the more-than-occasional mental health day. The school didn't even bother to call her house, since her parents were at the studio all day, and when you're a celebrity—even a local one—the rules were different for you and your offspring.

The rest of my morning classes were uneventful as I moved through the halls and into the cafeteria, taking stock of the huge crowd in there. I was starving, but as I looked at the packed tables, I was losing my appetite rapidly.

Without Hope and our—or, her—gang, I had no one to eat lunch with. I had friends before Hope, but she never liked them, and I never bothered to stand up for them when Hope made fun of them so they were long gone now.

I slid my tray along the lunch line, selecting the least gray-looking hamburger and a paper cup of limp french fries.

"Aw, it's our poet literette."

I had drunk beers with Rustin Rice in his backyard over Labor Day before Hope ripped my heart out. He was an idiot but an all-right guy—or he was before he thunked into me, slamming the edge of his tray hard into my left kidney, his soda sloshing from the cup and onto my T-shirt. He laughed at his own stupid, poorly worded joke.

"Hey, Rice," I said, my words barely audible through my gritted teeth.

"Write any good poems lately?"

The kids in the lunch line behind Rice—a couple of girls we ate lunch with, a few underclassmen, and a kid I didn't recognize—laughed with him, and I could feel the heat sear my cheeks. I hope it looked like anger rather than niggling embarrassment that wouldn't go away. I threw my money down to the lunch lady and popped my earbuds into my ears, trying to drown out the peals of laughter.

I could still hear them.

I dumped my food in the nearest trash can, my stomach turning over on itself, and made a beeline to the front hallway. Two girls I recognized—Renee, from class, and her friend Everly—were standing shoulder to shoulder, leaning into each other and whispering furiously. They stopped when they saw me, each eyeing me without trying to hide it.

I gave them a slight nod of my head. "Hey."

Renee looked disgusted. "Hey? Is that all you have to say for yourself?"

"Hey…Renee?"

She grunted. Everly gave a little snort. "You know that Hope's not here today, right?" Renee said, hands on hips, lips pressed in an accusatory line.

I shrugged. "Yeah, I noticed. She sick or something?"

Now Renee snorted and Everly grunted. "Like you don't know. You know she was being stalked, right?" She narrowed her eyes. "Of course you know. You were responsible."

"I wasn't stalking Hope. She was my girlfriend."

"Yeah," Everly said matter-of-factly. "And then she dumped you."

I nodded, happy to let them believe whatever Hope had told them. "Yeah, it happens. No big deal."

"So, she dumps you. Then, like a day later, she's getting prank phone calls, pizza sent to her house at all hours, random, disgusting stuff sent to her...adult diapers and crap like that." Renee was on a roll.

I tried to hide my head as I grinned and loosely congratulated myself. Wrong move as it apparently incensed Renee.

"Oh, you think that's funny? How did all these people get her phone number, Tony? Or her address?"

I felt my face flush but tried to ignore it, tried to stay calm. "I don't know. One of those star maps?" I grinned; Renee gaped.

"Celebrities get hacked all the time, and Hope pretty much fancies herself a celebrity, right? Comes with the territory. She should have been more careful, I guess."

Renee looked like she was about to explode, but Everly caught my eye and gave me a small smile before looking away. She thought it was funny too.

"Besides, this isn't the first time Hope hasn't shown up at school. She's probably home lying on the couch." I turned, ready to head down the hall.

"Except that she's not," Renee said, her voice stark. "Her mother called me and asked if I'd seen Hope. Obviously she's not home on the couch if her own mother doesn't know where she is."

I paused at this, a tiny prickle of guilt itching the back of my neck. *Was she home at all last night?* I took a deep breath. Even if she wasn't, it didn't mean anything. I thought of the crushed gutter phone, the one that was now stashed in my glove box. This was Hope, the girl who left nothing to chance. She had a million hiding places and three credit cards. While most kids drank a few beers in the supermarket parking lot to get away, Hope rented a hotel room or went to the Bahamas or holed up in a dressing room at Nordstrom. She wasn't exactly the down-and-out type.

"I'm sure Hope is just fine," I muttered before leaving.

But unease lit in my gut, and I couldn't seem to shake it.

SIX

By the end of the school day, Hope was all anyone was talking about. I hadn't spoken to anyone other than during my unfortunate run-ins with Renee and Everly, but everyone seemed to know something. There was a phone call, or I was the last to see or talk to her, or that she was "really scared" of "something or someone" who had contacted her.

The scandal had all the markings of a Hope scheme. Her friends seemed to be the most in the know, but also were spitting out little morsels of information when it suited them. Every time I passed Renee or Ashleigh on my way to class or in the hall, they shredded me with their razor-blade stares or immediately got on their rhinestone-studded phones and started whispering frantically.

It wouldn't be the first time Hope had exacted revenge. When she lost out for editor of the school newspaper, she had her parents donate enough money to start the school news channel—with herself as primary anchor. Her first story was an exposé on the journalism teacher, highlighting his DUI arrest.

When she lost out for homecoming queen, Hope threw a wild,

over-the-top party at the same time as the dance so the homecoming queen was crowned with an empty court and exactly six people on the dance floor. Hope could be sweet, smart, and funny—as long as you didn't cross her—and boy, did she love a good revenge.

When the Florence High newscast flashed across the flat panels in sixth period, the headline news was *Where Is Hope?* I had rolled my eyes. She had been gone less than a day. Some of the students in class were rapt, sitting up and watching the newscast. Other kids had barely looked up from their laptop or phone or book, and one kid—Lance Hutchings, a fringe burner no one paid attention to—actually snorted and rolled his eyes.

"She probably stayed home with a yeast infection or something," he muttered, crossing his arms in front of his chest and sliding low in his desk. "Why is a sick chick news?"

Renee—we were lucky to be in nearly every class together—shot him one of the looks I thought she only reserved for me and growled.

"She's been missing almost twenty-four hours. She didn't come home last night, you miscreant. She's not home sick, she's *missing*." Renee positively hissed the word, and I strangled a laugh in my throat. Yep, orchestrated. Straight out of a Hope's *Leave 'Em Wanting More* playbook.

Lance rolled his eyes again. "If it were anyone else in this class, no one would give a crap. It sure wouldn't make the news." He raised a dismissive hand, letting everyone knew how he felt about the caliber of Florence High School's reporting.

Renee narrowed her eyes. "And where were you last night, *Lance?*"

He waggled his eyebrows. "Maybe you should ask your friend Hope."

The newscast then flashed to a special message, and even I straightened in my seat. The Jensens. Looking distraught and uncomfortable, perched on the very edges of their fancily upholstered morning show chairs. The camera tightened its angle on the couple.

"As some of you know, our daughter, Hope, a junior at your high school, didn't come home last night," Bruce started.

Becky nodded next to him, wide-eyed and serious. She cleared her throat and licked her lips.

"Hope has always checked in with us, has always been open and honest with us. At this point, she's not answering her cell phone and has not been active on social media since eight p.m. last night."

"If you have any information that might be pertinent—even if it doesn't seem like anything important, please, please contact us or the police." I dazed out as a number flashed on the screen.

"A car that you didn't recognize at school, or someone on campus perhaps? Maybe you had a conversation with Hope that seemed"—Becky shrugged her tiny shoulders—"different somehow?"

I didn't have to turn around to know that everyone was staring at me.

"Didn't Hope and Tony have a"—a kid who sat behind me made air quotes—"*different* kind of conversation the other day?"

There was a round of low laughter, cut by Renee's sneer. "This is serious!"

"Tony and Hope broke up," Everly said carefully, and I wasn't sure if she was on my side or not. "It happens."

"Yeah, and two days later Hope goes missing."

Anger and guilt sat like flat stones in the pit of my stomach. "What exactly are you trying to say, Renee?"

Renee crossed her arms in front of her chest and popped her lip out in that mean-girl way that I'm pretty sure Hope had coined. She didn't say anything; she didn't have to. Accusation wafted from her.

The whole class was silent for an agonizing minute that seemed to stretch on. I jumped when Lance clapped a hand on my back. "Looks like you're about to be famous, dude."

By the time we were dismissed from class, the student body had grown into one pulsing mass, talking, whispering, pointing, staring at me. I kept my head down, trying to make a straight line for the student lot and my car, but there were people everywhere.

"That's Tony Gardner," I heard a shrill voice yelling. "He's Hope's ex-boyfriend."

When I looked up, I saw that it was Renee, talking to a police officer. My temperature ratcheted up, but the officer just looked at me and nodded, jotting something down in his notebook.

I got in my car just as I saw the Channel 7 news van pull into the school's horseshoe-shaped parking lot.

"Looks like you're about to be famous, dude."

SEVEN

The gossip and stares were worse the second day. People were convinced Hope wasn't just missing but that she'd actually been kidnapped. If you listened to the rumors, the gossip, she had been snatched and sold into white slavery or ended up as serial killer fodder, or had been taken by Colombians for a hefty ransom. She had skipped town due to drugs, run off with an Internet boyfriend or a Tunisian prince; someone's cousin had spotted her in Hawaii or the Barbados; she had been working on her GED and was recruited by Quantico.

"We just want her back safely," Renee wailed in biology class.

No one talked to me, but everyone was talking about me.

"The boyfriend did it," someone muttered as I stood at my locker.

"I thought the butler always did it," someone else guffawed.

"Who else was mad at Hope?"

Everyone, I wanted to scream. *Hope burned everyone. That was how she operated.*

She was the celebrity darling, the princess of Florence High. She had followers and admirers and flatterers, and when she loved you, she loved you fiercely with all her heart and soul and bank accounts and privilege, but when she was through with you…

Our love is a flower…

When Hope Jensen was through with you, she wouldn't just discard you, she needed to destroy you. She loved revenge. She loved *teaching a lesson* to anyone she presumed wronged her. That was Hope. She needed entrails in her wake. She needed a trail of broken hearts to prove that her own heart was worthwhile, and she would do whatever she could to get the outcome she wanted.

* * *

When I pulled up to the elementary school, Alice was sitting outside on one of the long benches with the rest of her class. My kid sister is in second grade, and although I know I'm supposed to find her sticky and annoying (and a lot of the time she is), I still think she's wickedly cute and funny for being such a little squirt. She broke into a huge smile when she saw my car and came running toward me, a construction paper butterfly taped to a paint stirrer in one hand, a mass of all her second-grade necessities in the other. I took her lunch box, her backpack, and her jacket and shoved it all into the backseat while she flapped the construction paper butterfly around for a minute before climbing into her booster chair.

"Hi, Tony!"

"Hey, squirt, did you have a good day?"

Alice worked the belts on her booster seat. She was still a peanut; her nose barely reached the window. "I'm not the squirt, you're the squirt," she said, using the butterfly as a pointer.

"Okay, fine," I said, palms up. "I'm the squirt. How was your day? Were you a good kid?"

I gunned the engine and pulled out of the parking lot while Alice's butterfly caught the wind that whooshed through the back window.

"See my butterfly?"

I glanced in the rearview mirror and caught Alice's eye. "I sure do. Is that for Mom?"

"Nuh-uh." Alice shook her head furiously. "Guess again."

"Dad?"

"Nope."

I slapped a palm against my heart. "Me? Aw, you shouldn't have!"

"I didn't. It's for Hope." Alice grinned, little-kid teeth sharp and uneven against her pink lips. "For when she comes back."

My tongue went heavy in my mouth. "What are you talking about, Alice?"

She continued to fly her insect across the backseat. "'Cuz Hope is gone right now, and when she comes back home…" Alice grinned at me and popped me on the top of the head with the butterfly. "It's for welcome."

I swallowed slowly, my stomach rolling into tight knots. "How do you know Hope is gone?"

"Some mommies were talking about it at my school. Someone said Hope got a nap, and someone said that she just runned away."

"A nap?" I mutter to myself.

Kidnapped.

"Hope doesn't like to run though," Alice continued. "It makes her sparkle."

* * *

I was at home long enough to flip through all the channels and see that Hope's story was being reported on three of them. All the reports were vague at best, some reporting things like suspicious circumstances but never saying what those circumstances were. I shifted on the couch and flicked the TV to cartoons when Alice came padding in from the kitchen, her little face serious as she balanced an overfilled bowl of cereal and milk. She eyed me and took a huge spoonful.

"Ma said I could eat this."

I shrugged, just glad that Alice hadn't seen the newscast and happy that my parents were at work so they wouldn't have been able to see it either. I figured it would blow over by tomorrow morning—Friday, at the latest, Hope making some big appearance and the whole school still laughing at me.

But the cops were involved...

And then the doorbell rang.

Alice looked at me, a wad of Fruity Pebbles mounded in her cheek. "Who's that?"

I opened the door and stepped in front of Alice. Flashes went off, and I tried to blink away the hot, black spots.

There are two uniformed officers on my doorstep, and behind them, what seemed to be a sea of reporters tramping on our lawn and shoving their iPhones in front of them, snippets of flashes bursting in the twilight.

"Tony Gardner?" the female officer asked me.

I nodded dumbly.

"I'm Officer MacNamara, and this is Officer Pace. Are your parents home, son?"

Pace nodded his head, and I nodded to both of them. I've never had a run-in with cops before, never had any bad feelings toward them, but then again, I've never had a pair on my front porch asking my name and if my parents were home. I didn't know what to say to them.

"Uh, they're not home yet."

There was an awkwardly long pause while Pace and MacNamara seemed to expect something from me. Numbly, I stepped aside, waved my arm, and then they were in my living room, a male and a female cop, him slim and broad shouldered under his black shirt, her straight from shoulder to ankle. MacNamara closed the door on the flashes and the screaming mob.

"What's going on? Why... When did they get here?"

Pace looked absently over his shoulder and shrugged. "They're just looking for a scoop."

I nodded, still not entirely understanding. I peeked out the peephole on the door. There were only three reporters and two cameramen, but our yard was small, and having never had a single newsperson on the lawn, it looked like a paparazzi zoo.

"Are they allowed to be here?"

Officer Pace waved a hand. "Not on the lawn. They have to stay down on the sidewalk."

I glanced out the inch of window visible through the blinds and noticed that no one was on the sidewalk, that the reporters were tangled on the lawn, one leaning up against the orange tree that has never actually produced an orange.

"We'll get rid of them on our way out."

I nodded, still feeling dumb, feeling out of place in my own house.

Alice pulled against my pant leg, pulled the back of my jeans. I had almost forgotten she was there. She tried to peer around me, but I inched her back again, crouched down low and told her to go to her room. She stared up at the police officers.

"Are you here for Hope?" she asked, her voice thin and babyish, and I wished she'd just go in her room.

MacNamara crouched down next to me and Alice and smiled kindly.

"We're here to bring Hope home," she said. "What's your name?"

I stood up and stepped in front of Alice again. I don't want her to be a part of this, of any of this.

"Go watch TV in Mom and Dad's room, Alice."

Alice thankfully did as she was told, and I crossed my arms in front of my chest and stared down MacNamara. I was not nervous until the other officer, Pace, stepped in front of me. He jutted a chin toward Alice.

"She yours?"

I blinked, looking toward the hallway, then back again. "Alice? She's my kid sister."

"So no kids?"

I couldn't tell if he was joking, but I thought it best not to laugh. "No, sir."

"We'd just like to ask you a few questions, Tony. Is that okay?" It was MacNamara now. Her voice was calm and serene, just like her smile.

"Don't my parents need to be here or something?"

Pace shrugged like we were all friends.

"We're not here to interrogate you, if that's what you're concerned about. We just have some questions about the night Hope went missing that we're hoping you can clear up for us. If you'd like to wait until your parents come home, we can certainly do that."

Neither MacNamara nor Pace looked like they were planning to wait anywhere but in my living room so I shrugged and gestured toward the kitchen table.

"S'okay, I guess. Want to sit?"

They did and Pace pulled a little notebook out of his breast pocket, a little leather-bound thing that I'd seen every cop on every TV show ever pull out. I wondered if they were standard issue like gun belts or badges.

"So Tony, did you speak to Hope two nights ago?"

I tore my eyes from the little notebook and blinked at MacNamara. She didn't blink back. Her eyes were flat, wide saucers that weren't intimidating but weren't friendly either.

"Uh, yeah. She called me around nine."

"And how did she sound?"

Annoyed. Frustrated... Worried.

I licked my paper-dry lips. "I don't know. Regular, I guess. Then maybe...a little worried."

MacNamara raised her eyebrows. "Worried?" she asked.

I nodded. I folded my hands in my lap, gripping so hard my palms immediately started to sweat.

"Well, yeah. I mean, annoyed at first, then a little worried, I guess."

Pace looked up from the notebook he was writing in. "And that didn't bother you?"

I swallowed. "Sir?"

"Bother you? You didn't think you should do anything about it?"

"About her tone of voice?" I didn't intend to, but I felt myself shrugging again. "Hope…gets worked up. She's kind of emotional so…"

A smile cracked across Pace's face. "Women, huh?"

I feel my cheeks redden, and I glanced at MacNamara who either wasn't listening or didn't care.

"I guess. I mean, we were fighting. She wasn't exactly happy with me."

"Because you had just broken up?" MacNamara clarified.

I shifted in my seat. "Yeah, that's why."

"But she broke up with you, isn't that right?"

I heard Hope's voice echo in the back of my head, smug: *Our love is a flower that blooms…*"

"No. I broke up with her."

Neither of the cops looked convinced, and my whole body tensed. I hoped the cops couldn't see it. I cleared my throat and put my hands on the table. I saw some cop show once that said people who hid their hands tended to hide other things too. I didn't want the cops to ask me any more questions. I wanted them to think I was being totally honest.

I *was* being totally honest.

The computer screen flashed in my mind's eye. The websites,

Hope's information, the smiling picture of her in her red-and-white-striped bikini top, her breasts pressed halfway to her chin.

Share Location?

That blinking cursor.

I felt the sweat break out at my forehead, could feel a bead break free and drip down the center of my back. My heart started to thump, and I was sure everyone could hear it: Pace, MacNamara, the goons with the flashing cameras outside, Hope.

Where was Hope?

"Have you found her? Have you been looking for Hope?" My voice came out low and raspy, creepy even in my own ears. I cleared my throat.

MacNamara actually looked sorry for me. She put her hand on my arm, her five fingers burning like five cattails into my flesh. "We're doing the best we can, Tony. We're going to find her, and we're going to bring her back home safe and in one piece." She kind of smiled, but it didn't reach her eyes. "That's why we're here today, covering all of our bases. You want us to find Hope too, don't you, Tony?"

I hated how she said my name, like she already owned it, like she had already arrested me, sentenced me, thrown me in jail.

"You want Hope to come home, don't you, Tony?"

I sat with lips pursed, willing myself to talk, unable to make it happen.

There was a commotion at the door, a fresh *rat-a-tat-tat* of camera-phone flashes and people yelling, and then my parents shimmied through the door, looking flushed and nervous. Their eyes darted from me to MacNamara to Pace. Alice came out of the bedroom, dressed in her shiny *Frozen* nightgown.

"Of course I want Hope to come home," I whispered.

* * *

The cops had been gone for barely two hours when the news reports continued streaming: *Daughter of Bruce and Becky Jensen Gone Missing. Where is Hope Jensen?* It was on every channel—there, then gone in a flash, Hope's smiling face almost immediately replaced by a stock photograph of the whole Jensen family looking television perfect in a panorama of carefully matched outfits, propped in front of a white sand beach in Florida or Myrtle Beach or probably some beach set that folded back up in the Channel 7 offices.

My mom fixed dinner, but I didn't move from the head of the table where my dad usually sat. He walked to a different chair and we ate in silence, the background noise from the television making my stomach lurch.

"They're going to find her," my mother said, her hand soft on my arm.

I nodded without looking at her. I couldn't say anything because I couldn't believe that Hope was actually missing. Girls like Hope didn't go missing. They ran the world. They made you fall in love with them; they tore your heart out of your chest and spat on it.

"Our love is a flower that blooms…"

I pushed my plate away.

She's not really missing.

It was Hope...trying to teach me a lesson.

A lump grew in my throat. Another news report: same story, different picture of perfect-looking Hope. My chest tightened; my skin felt like it was suddenly too tight.

"Can I be excused?" I asked.

I didn't wait for anyone to answer, because before they could, I was in the bathroom, the few bites of dinner that I did eat coming out in a stomach-torturing torrent. My head was pounding, and the sweat was blurring my eyes—sweat, or maybe tears. I didn't stay around to find out because my mother came in and pressed a wet compress to my forehead. She guided me across the hall and into my bedroom and gently pushed me down, taking off my shoes like she still did to Alice and pulling the covers up to my chest. I tried to open my eyes to look at her or thank her or apologize for being such a horrible son, but my room went dark and she shut the door with a soft puff of air behind her.

I didn't know how long I lay there. I didn't know if I slept. All I know is that the room was pitch-black when I opened my eyes, and my heart still felt like it was being squeezed. Where the guilt used to be was anger now, white and hot because Hope did this. Hope orchestrated this whole thing. She had to. Her whole life was orchestrated. Everything she did was to get the biggest shock, the biggest surprise, the biggest bang for her selfish buck.

I kicked off my blankets, pulled my phone off the charger, hit speed dial, and waited for Hope to pick up. I knew her phone was in my car, but figured for sure she would have the calls forwarded to whatever new phone or burner she'd procured because she was faking it. She had to be. Pulling a prank of this magnitude—going missing, making the world look for her while looking at me like some sort of criminal? It had Hope written all over it.

"Hi, you've reached Hope! Leave me a message!" Her voice was singsongy, every sentence ending with an exclamation point.

"Call me back, Hope. Pick up your goddamn phone and call me back. This isn't funny anymore. The police were here today." I gritted my teeth. "Call me, Hope."

I cut the phone off, then immediately dialed her again, not sure what I thought would happen. Two rings. Voice mail.

"Hi, you've reached Hope!"

I dialed again.

One ring.

Two ring.

A weird sound like fumbling, like someone trying to answer.

"Hope!"

"Hi, you've reached Hope…"

I threw my windbreaker over my head and went out the front door. The reporters were gone, but still I pushed my crap car down the driveway and halfway down the block so as not to wake my parents or Alice. It was amazing that Hope would allow herself to be seen with me in this heap. I got in, revved the engine, and sped out, headlights barely making a dent through the dense fog.

I didn't care where Hope was hiding. I was going to find her if it was the last thing I did. I was going to find her, and the whole world would know what a bitch she was—a manipulative little bitch.

I'm not your toy, Hope. I'm not your fucking plaything.

EIGHT

I didn't really know where I was going. It's not like Hope had some secret spot she would run off to or anything. Or, if she did, she kept it really well hidden because I had no idea where to go.

Instead, I found myself moving in the direction of Hope's house. I wasn't really thinking when I flicked on the blinker and took the left turn a little faster than I should. My tires squealed, and I tried to hug the road to keep control—my palms were sweating again— and then I heard the little *chirp-chirp* of the police car. I didn't even realize I was being followed. I pulled over, sighed, and grabbed my license and registration from the glove box. I tried to remember if I was speeding, but three minutes ago seemed like three lifetimes ago, and I couldn't even remember if I stopped at the four-way on Lupin two blocks back.

The police officer seemed to take forever getting out of his car. I couldn't see him clearly due to the thick yellow beam coming from his Maglite. He shined it through the driver's side window as I was rolling it down, and I was nearly blinded. When I could see again, I was staring into Officer Pace's face.

He didn't smile at me.

"Hello, Tony."

My throat was dry, even though now I was certain I didn't do anything wrong. "Here's my license and registration," I say anyway, holding them out to him.

Pace shook his head, waved a black-gloved hand at my open window. "That's not necessary. Where are you going at this time of night?"

I wasn't doing anything wrong, but my heart twisted in my chest. A thousand lies rolled through my head: *tell him you're getting Alice medicine, or your dad fell off a ladder, or your mom needs a cup of sugar.*

Instead, I heard myself say, "I'm looking for Hope."

Pace's dark eyebrows popped up. "Are you? And where are you planning to find her?"

I looked up the dark street and then back at Pace. "I don't really know, sir. I was just starting to drive."

"Looks to me like you're headed over to the Jensens' house."

I licked my lips. "Is that okay?"

"You think Hope's there?"

A little bubble of anger welled and popped in my chest. *I don't know where the hell Hope is,* I wanted to scream, *but I'm pretty sure she's screwing with all of us!*

"I don't know."

Pace sighed, crossed his arms in front of his chest, and spread his legs a little bit. The action wasn't cop-like. It was more *Let's be buddies and just chat.* I think I would have preferred cop-like.

"Hope was a lot of work, wasn't she, Tony?"

I didn't answer for a beat, and Pace went on. "I mean, dating her wasn't that easy, right? She seemed like she would have been pretty high maintenance. Maybe even a little bitchy?"

I wanted to agree with him because yeah, Hope could be a total bitch, and I wouldn't be on the side of the road at 3:00 a.m. on a Wednesday night if Hope wasn't high maintenance. But I knew what he was doing. I have seen a lot of cop shows.

"She isn't a hard person to date," I said carefully.

Pace cocked a brow. "So you're still dating?"

"No, but she isn't...like you're saying."

"Come on." Pace showed me the palms of his gloved hands. "It's not like this is going in the official report or anything. I'm just curious. I mean, the girls I dated in high school? They sure as hell didn't look like Hope, you know? And famous parents, always had TV cameras around, the best of everything..." Pace took a few steps away from the side of my car and eyed it, doing nothing to hide how unimpressed he was. "And you're just...well, you know. Regular. Like me, right? We're just regular guys."

"I guess."

"I'm just thinking maybe a girl like Hope, pretty worldly or whatever, maybe she thought she could fix you or take advantage of you. Or, maybe she kind of made you feel shitty. She had a brand-new SUV, right? Bet you had to work your ass off for this hunk of—"

"Hope didn't even know how to drive." I didn't want to be friends with Pace. I knew he didn't want to be my therapist or some kind of father figure, that he was only trying to get me to talk so I'd say something incriminating, but it just kind of tumbled out.

Hope's parents got her the exact SUV she cut out of a dealer catalog and slapped on the refrigerator door. She had never talked about wanting a car or even learning to drive; I don't even know if she had her permit. But, one day we were at her place watching TV and a commercial came on: that SUV, roaring down some windy, ocean-lined highway. I told her I wanted that car. She said we could drive down the coast—whatever coast that was—and stay in a bed-and-breakfast or a bungalow or something like that. That it would be romantic. Just the two of us.

Two weeks later, the car was parked in her driveway with a bow.

"That must have made you mad, huh?"

I shifted in my seat. "Not mad, it was just…whatever, you know?"

"I don't know. That would piss me off. If I'm working my ass off for everything I have, and she just snaps her little fingers and *poof*! Everything you ever wanted."

"Hope isn't like that."

Hope was *exactly* like that.

"Oh, I'm not saying anything bad about her. I heard she was a real sweet girl. I'm just saying where it could make a guy mad."

I gripped my steering wheel. "Hope *is* a real sweet girl."

It wasn't exactly a lie.

Pace shrugged. "I'm just saying I could understand that kind of thing getting to you."

"It doesn't."

I was immediately pulled into a memory of me and Hope at the mall. It was Christmastime and we were shopping, and Hope was pouting because I wouldn't tell her what I wanted for Christmas. Not that I wouldn't tell her—it was just that I didn't really want anything. It was more like I wanted everything. I wanted the new snowboard jacket she pointed out, but I'd never even been to the snow, and I sure as hell couldn't afford a snowboard. I wanted the Bose noise-canceling headphones that she plopped on my head, but they were four hundred dollars. I couldn't have my girlfriend buy me a four-hundred-dollar gift when I had one hundred and seventy-two dollars to my name, and that was supposed to buy Hope, Mom, Dad, and Alice's gifts, plus pay my car insurance.

Hope put her hands on her hips, pushed out her bottom lip, and tapped one foot impatiently on the ugly mall tile floor. "Well, Tony Gardner, you're just no fun at all, are you? If you don't tell me what you want, you're going to end up with a lump of coal."

"Maybe I don't need anything because I've got everything I need right here." I snaked Hope into my arms and hugged her to me, and she melted, cuddling right up to me, her head nestling against my neck.

"You're so sweet," she cooed.

Now when I thought about that time at the mall, I wondered if there were cameras hidden somewhere—in the plastic play park or the fake snowdrifts in Santa's Workshop. I wonder if Hope was miked, something tucked under her sweatshirt or poking out of her jacket pocket. I can't remember if that piece of our life made it on the show, but something tells me if it wasn't a vignette surrounded by fake snow and Christmas music, it was at least retold by Bruce and Becky on one of their hundred Christmas specials.

"Like I said…" Pace went on, actually kicking at the asphalt like he was nervous or shy or something a cop shouldn't be. "It would be understandable if you just lost it one day…"

A coil of anger worked its way through me, and I prayed that Pace couldn't see my knuckles turn white as I gripped the steering wheel.

"I didn't do anything to Hope. If that's what you were wondering, why didn't you just ask me? I don't know where Hope is. I didn't have anything do to with what happened to her."

Pace was unfazed. "And what happened to Hope, Tony? Why do you start by telling me that?"

"I don't know what you want me to say. I don't know what happened to Hope, I promise. If anything happened to her at all. That's why I'm out here, I just thought—" I felt stupid, like I was playing right into Pace's hands, but I didn't know what else to do other than tell the truth. "I just thought maybe if I drove around, I could find her. Is that a crime?"

Pace actually chuckled. "You tell me, lover boy."

There was an edge to his voice now, the friendly "you can tell me anything" tone gone.

I sucked in a slow breath, focusing on the cracked leather on my steering wheel. "Am I under arrest?"

"Should you be?"

Another breath. "Right now. Am I under arrest, or can I go?"

Pace took a step back from the car and wiped his nonexistent fingerprints from my windshield with his elbow. "You're not under arrest. You're free to go whenever you like." He opened his arms like he had the key to the city. "Be my guest."

I grabbed my license and registration from my lap and went to cram them back in the glove box. I saw it the same instance Pace did. Hope's phone. He raised his eyebrows.

"That's quite a phone."

The thing was bedazzled with pink-and-white diamonds or rhinestones or whatever. Had a swirly pink *H* on it. Even though it was half shattered, this obviously wasn't my phone.

"Yours?"

I swallowed hard. Did I lie? My mind surged: Was it worse to be found with Hope's phone or to lie about having it? I palmed it. Handed it to Pace.

"I found it in the gutter when I went to Hope's that first night."

Pace turned the phone over in his hand. "You didn't think to mention it earlier?"

I shrugged. "I forgot." It sounded stupid and weak—fake even to me. "See…" I took the phone from him and swiped it open. "See, there are a bunch of missed calls from me. I was looking for her."

Pace glanced at the screen. "You have her pass code?"

"Uh…"

"What time did you say you found the phone?"

"I don't know…nine, ten maybe? After I talked to her, I went over to her house. I found the phone in the gutter."

Pace was nodding, going along with me. "So you picked it up, put it in your glove box, then went home and called Hope."

I nodded my head. "Yeah, that's exactly what happened."

Was Pace on my side?

"Why would you call Hope's phone when it was in your glove box, Tony? Why would you call a phone you knew Hope couldn't answer?"

My heart started to sink.

Heat burst out everywhere.

"I thought... I thought she would forward the calls." My voice was a hoarse whisper. "Maybe to a burner phone. She wanted me to find the phone."

Pace pinned me with a stare that said everything. He was careful to barely touch the phone, dropping it into a plastic bag he produced from his shirt pocket.

"Go home, Tony."

NINE

When I walked into the kitchen the following morning, Alice was already at the table with yet another bowl of cereal, her eyes glued to some cartoon on the iPad. My parents were moving silently and robotically, furtively glancing at the living room TV tuned to Channel 7 and the Jensens' morning show.

The show's music swelled, and the credits started to roll but then were immediately frozen. The familiar, jaunty *Wake Up the Bay!* tune was stunted, replaced by the tones usually reserved for breaking news—natural disasters, mass shootings, election coverage. Instead of being immediately sent by satellite to a major office in DC or New York City, the show opened with the normal Channel 7 news desk, the daily anchors looking serious and distraught.

"We're breaking into our regularly scheduled program to bring you this exclusive. Hope Jensen, seventeen, the daughter of Channel 7's own Bruce and Becky Jensen of *Wake Up the Bay!* is officially being declared a missing person. We go to the Florence County Police Department press conference already in progress."

The camera cut to an overbright shot of the white stucco front of the police department. The chief of police was gripping both sides of a wooden podium with big, meat-hook hands and staring out at the assembled crowd—mainly reporters with cell phones at the ready.

"At approximately eleven-oh-two p.m. on Monday night, Hope Jensen was having a phone conversation with a school friend. No one has seen or heard from Hope since. We are following every lead and taking this investigation very seriously. If you have any information…"

The police chief's voice was drowned out by a flurry of shouted questions and waving hands.

"Chief! Chief! Will you be divulging the name of the person with whom Hope was speaking?"

"Is that person a suspect?"

"What have you done so far?"

"Any leads that you can tell us about?"

The police chief looked at his audience before patting them down to silence with his big hands. "There will be a more formal press conference later this evening where we'll do our best to answer all your questions."

"Are you forming a search party?" The question was asked by someone in the front row who didn't bother to raise a hand or a microphone.

"Like I said, your questions will be answered in due time. Right now I'd like to present Mr. and Mrs. Jensen, who would like to speak to whoever might have Hope."

"So it is a kidnapping!" Another disembodied voice. A sharp look from the chief of police.

Bruce and Becky Jensen were shuffled to the front of the podium. They looked like a matched pair: he in his crisp navy suit, she in her white dress with navy piping, a thick belt cinching her tiny waist. Becky held a framed, close-up photo of Hope that the camera zoomed in on before pulling out to get Bruce and Becky's drawn faces in the shot. It was obvious they had been crying—the Hollywood kind that only leaves a heady trace of pink at the end of noses, that makes the eyes look dewy and watery rather than sunken and bloodshot.

"Hope, we want you to know that we love you very much, and we are praying and doing everything possible to ensure your safe return. We love you, baby."

Bruce clapped a hand over one of his wife's and squeezed obviously as they exchanged a tortured look. "If you have our daughter or know anything about her whereabouts, we implore you to contact us or let her go. There will be no questions asked. No follow-up, no consequences if you just bring our daughter home to us. Hope is our miracle, our special little angel. She wouldn't hurt anyone, and she deserves to be home with us, with her family. Please, please just let her go."

Bruce dissolved into tears, and the chief of police hurried them away from the crowd, whisking them into the police station. A second uniformed officer came to the podium.

I turned off the TV, pocketed my keys, and left the house without saying good-bye to anyone.

* * *

School was humming when I got there. There were more reporters, more cops, more adults dressed in somber suits clutching clipboards to their chests and urging students to talk about their grief or their guilt or their feelings. Everyone seemed to be focused on themselves, little ants walking in lines until I got there. Then, like I'd shown up with a marching band, everyone turned and looked. No expression on their faces except for something that looked like curiosity but only lasted a moment. And then I could see it. Eyes darkening. Lips twitching. Heads bending, hands cupping mouths, the whispers starting.

"Tony was the last one to see Hope alive…"

"You never know what people are capable of…"

"Do you think he could have…"

The whispers were deafening roars. The stares, the way their eyes burned. Accusation was everywhere. *Tony did it. Tony is responsible. Hope is dead, Hope is gone, something horrible has happened to Hope, and it's all Tony's fault.*

I was no longer the loser, the pansy, the oversensitive sap.

I was a murderer.

"Mr. Gardner, Tony, Tony!" A man in a suit who I didn't recognize was leading the pack of adults calling my name. He wasn't a cop, wasn't a reporter—at least he didn't have a microphone in his hand. He cut in front of the rest and made a beeline for me, clamping a hand over my arm and leaning uncomfortably close.

"Don't say a word to any of them."

"What? Who are you?"

The man in the suit steered me to the side of the school where the lunch tables were, holding his hand out behind him, stop-sign style. The advancing reporters, students, and cops actually stopped as though this guy wielded some kind of power over them. I stiffened and shook off his arm.

"Do I know you?"

The guy guided me to a table and presented me with a business card in one fluid motion.

Alfred Bellingham, Attorney at Law.

"I don't need an attorney." I attempted to hand the card back, but Bellingham refused it, looking everywhere but at me before he sat down.

"With all due respect, kid, you do. I've already left a message with your parents. Since you're a minor, you can't enter into any legal contracts with me without your parents' consent. But Tony, the press and these cops are already doing a number on you. You need me. Do you have a lawyer yet?"

I couldn't imagine that my parents would know where to find a lawyer, let alone this guy who'd seemed to appear out of nowhere.

"I don't think I should be talking to you." I left the card on the table and stood up, not exactly sure where I was headed. The reporters were chomping at the edge of the lunch tables, and Bellingham was behind me. The kids that were my friends last week were milling around, pretending not to pay attention, to care, but I could see their eyebrows raised, could see their eyes cut to me and back to one another before the whispering began again.

"You know they have blood evidence," Bellingham said nonchalantly.

I stopped, his words dripping over me like slime. My skin started to crawl. "Blood?"

"Hope's."

I turned slowly. The cops hadn't mentioned a thing. I thought of Hope, of her full, bloodred lips slightly parted as she threw her head back and laughed.

"They found Hope's blood?" My stomach folded in on itself, and I gripped the cemented edges of the lunch table, my head, everything, starting to spin. "Does that mean she's—"

Bellingham shook his head. "No, from what I hear they're trace amounts, but the cops can spin it any which way, Tony. You need someone to protect you, protect your rights. You were the last to speak to her, right?"

"I-I... We were on the phone. How do they even know who—?"

Bellingham shrugged like it was common knowledge. "Phone records. Easy enough to get. Or they probably just found her phone."

"No, I—" I paused and bit my lip, but Bellingham didn't seem to react.

"Well, look. I'm not saying you're a suspect right now. Neither are the police. But you're the ex-boyfriend..."

I stiffened. "Hope's not dead."

Bellingham went palms up again, placating me like he had the press. "Of course not, of course not. No one's saying that. You just need to be prepared, Tony. They could come after you. And when they do, they're going to want to impound your car and come back to your house with a search warrant. I'm not saying you did anything wrong, but you could be in some serious trouble."

I swallowed hard, my teeth gritted. "Did the cops send you? Do they want me to talk to you?"

Then Bellingham stood up and came uncomfortably close again. "I'm on your side, Tony. I want what you want. I want to get Hope back safely, to get to the bottom of this and prosecute who took her. But you need to be protected."

"And you're going to do that? Protect me?"

Bellingham shrugged, the sheen of his suit catching on the early-morning sun. "I want to try." He pinched the business card I left on the table between his first two fingers and held it out to me. "Why don't you have your parents give me a call at their earliest convenience?"

I hesitated, but took the card. It was heavy, with raised blue lettering and the scales of justice printed in blue and gold on the right-hand side. I couldn't look at him. "Why do you want to help me? You don't even know me."

"I want to help Hope, just like you do. And I think the best way to do that is to help you. I don't think you have anything to do with any of this." He gestured vaguely, and I wasn't sure if he meant Hope, the school, or the throng of cops and reporters. "And it's important to me as an attorney to see that justice is served." He pinned me with a gaze and sucked in a short breath. "For you and for Hope. Call me, okay?"

Without waiting for a reply, Bellingham nodded curtly, turned on his fancy wing-tipped shoes, and walked with intent directly toward the reporters and cops. Phones were flung forward, microphones pressed in his face, cameras flashing.

"Mr. Bellingham! Mr. Bellingham!" The reporters seemed to know exactly who he was. "Is it true that Tony Gardner has retained counsel? Will you be taking Tony's case? Have the police instructed Mr. Gardner to retain counsel? Is he a suspect in this case?"

I watched as Bellingham expertly hushed the crowd.

"Mr. Bellingham! Does you being here confirm that Tony Gardner is indeed a suspect in Hope Jensen's disappearance? Is he officially being called a suspect? Has he made any statements?"

The police officers wordlessly tried to push back the reporters, to edge a path for Mr. Bellingham. The reporters ignored the police and leaned in toward Bellingham, microphones and iPhones extended, ready to catch every word. I felt myself leaning in too, my breath tight in my throat.

Mr. Bellingham looked to the crowd, then back at me.

"I have no comment on the situation," he said.

TEN

I was a pariah at school. No one talked to me; everyone just stared. The teachers took an extra-long time handing papers back to me. The administrators made a wide berth but didn't say anything. They just kept staring.

When the classroom emptied out after the lunch bell, Mr. Henry sat on the desk across from me.

"You know, you're welcome to eat your lunch in here," he said casually. "If you want a little break."

I looked up, grateful. "Thank you."

He jutted his chin toward the still-open door, toward the masses swarming the halls. "High school is just a microcosm of the world. Passing judgment without any actual proof of anything."

I shifted, suddenly aware of how uncomfortably hard the desk chairs were. "Yeah."

"So far all we know is that Hope is missing, right?"

"Yeah, I guess that's what the police are saying."

"They don't even know if a crime has actually been committed then."

I blinked.

"You know… Was she kidnapped? Did she take off on her own? Kids do that. Teenagers, especially. Runaways."

"I guess. Hope didn't really have anything to run away from." I thought of her house, the pristine yard, the enormous swimming pool. Hope had everything. Why would she run?

To teach me a lesson.

I pushed the salami sandwich I packed for myself back on the desk.

"Did they find anything out about her?" Mr. Henry leaned forward then, arms crossed in front of his chest, ankles crossed so that his khaki pants rode up, exposing his purple-and-black argyle socks. "You know, if maybe she was seeing someone local"—he shrugged, his sweater vest bunching around his shoulders— "or maybe she met someone online. Took off to be with him or something. You read about that kind of stuff all the time."

I just nodded, my eye wandering to the two girls in the school hallway unfurling a banner.

Mr. Henry rambled on, but I'd stopped listening.

Renee held one end of the sign while Ashleigh unrolled it, taking careful backward steps. It made a huge racket. The thing seemed about three feet wide by a thousand feet long, painted over with thick paint that made the paper bubble and crunch. I watched Renee pull off a hunk of masking tape and smooth the poster on the wall. Painted in big, fat green letters were the words: WE'LL NEVER STOP LOOKING FOR YOU, HOPE!

Ashleigh pasted a huge photograph of Hope on either

side—Hope with her head thrown back, grinning, and Hope with the glinting eyes and soft expression she used when she wanted something. The second picture was alluring. If I hadn't seen that exact expression, didn't know about the hard cut to her eyes just before she innocently batted them at me, I would have marched into the hall and fallen to my knees, begging Renee and Ashleigh to let me help find Hope.

"I'm not saying we shouldn't be worried." Mr. Henry was walking around the classroom, picking things up and putting them down again. "I'm just saying it's a little early for so much alarm, don't you think?"

"What?" Mr. Henry was staring at me, and heat snaked up the back of my neck.

"Well, you knew Hope pretty well. You guys were dating, right?"

"I know Hope pretty well, yeah. But"—here I shifted, still weirdly embarrassed—"we broke up."

"Do you want to talk about it?"

I could still see Renee and Ashleigh just out of the corner of my eye. They were admiring their handiwork before Renee collapsed onto Ashleigh's shoulder, her body racking with sobs.

"Where is she?" Ashleigh cried.

Something inside my gut twisted hard, and the few bites of sandwich I did eat threatened to come back up. I swiped everything off my desk and into my backpack and gave Mr. Henry a quick glance.

"Thanks. I've got to go."

Students weren't allowed in the parking lot during school hours unless they were coming or going, so I hunkered down in the front seat of my car and let the sun beat down on me.

"God damn it, Hope."

I don't know how long I sat there, but it was long enough for the bell to ring and for kids to go back to class. It was long enough for a police cruiser to slowly come down the long, horseshoe-shaped driveway. I couldn't tell if the officers inside were Pace and MacNamara, but when the cruiser pulled into a faculty spot up front, I crouched down lower as the two officers got out. I could tell Pace by the slow, lumbering way he walked, and MacNamara by her quick, tight stride. They made a beeline for the principal's office.

I waited a full fifteen minutes for them to come out after me. When they didn't, I breathed slowly in and pulled Bellingham's card out of my pocket. I studied it and turned it over and over in my hand until it was damp and felt like cloth. When Pace and MacNamara left the office with Principal Jacobs between them, I pushed the car into gear and pulled my cell phone from my pocket.

* * *

Mr. Bellingham's office was nice inside with sleek leather furniture and one of those giant-leafed houseplants toppling out of a chrome canister. He had a secretary named Mirelle who sat at a small desk about fifteen feet in front of me. She was wearing a headset and tapping away. The whole thing looked very posh and professional.

"I'm glad you called, Tony," Mr. Bellingham said across from me, as he knit his hands over his stomach. "Do you want to wait for your parents?"

I shifted in the leather seat. I was sweating through my T-shirt, and the slick leather was making everything worse. "I actually haven't called them."

Bellingham leaned forward, and I stopped him. "I'll be eighteen in three weeks. I didn't think…" I looked away. "And I don't want to get them involved if I don't have to." I couldn't bear to think of my parents in this office, trying to get comfortable in these stupid new-age chairs, of Alice trying to make conversation with Mirelle, whose red-tipped fingernails hadn't stopped typing since I walked in.

"In order to get started, I will, in fact, need their permission as you are still a minor but"—Bellingham shook his head and did something like click his tongue or his teeth—"turning eighteen in three weeks isn't exactly the best place for you to be right now. Sorry about that."

I shrugged because what the hell else could I do?

"I just need… I didn't do—"

Bellingham held out a hand. "Here's the thing, Tony. This is a high-profile case. The media—and the Jensens especially—are putting a lot of pressure on the police department to get this thing solved as soon as possible. To get Hope home as soon as possible," he added as an obvious afterthought. "They're going to go for the most obvious suspect."

"Me."

"You were the last to talk to her."

"I saw her at school."

"Sure, yeah, of course. It's just in cases like these—lovers' spat, lady goes missing—more often than not…"

"I didn't do anything. I'm not guilty. You've got to believe me. I was pissed at Hope, but I would never do anything…never do anything to physically hurt her." I felt the tears rim my eyes, then start falling. I dug my fingernails into my palms, tightening my fists. "I didn't do anything, I swear to you."

Bellingham actually smiled. It was a weird, slick, satisfied smile that made my blood run cold and sent a shot of goose bumps up the wet spot between my shoulder blades.

"And that's exactly what the media needs to hear. That's what the jury needs to hear. They all need to know this guy." Bellingham held a hand out to me, and the tears dried abruptly.

"What?"

"This is the Tony the media needs to see. You have to get them to sympathize with you. Take a look at this." He flipped his computer screen around to show a frozen picture of Hope. It was yet another iteration of her smiling, this time a shy, sweet smile, the one she offered with wide, round eyes that a guy could get lost in. Bellingham hit a key, and as the news ticker ran across the bottom of the screen, the picture of Hope dissolved into a partially grainy home movie of Hope in a play, fifth grade from the looks of it. Her long, blond hair was braided into two pigtails, and she was dressed as Dorothy from *The Wizard of Oz*. She was gripping her blue gingham skirt and rocking from side to side, singing about rainbows and yellow brick roads.

"Sweet. Innocent. Gotta find this kid, right?" Bellingham was asking.

I nodded because I didn't know what else to do.

The clip of Hope as Dorothy disappeared and was replaced by a hard-looking newswoman ticking off a list of things that I'd heard Hope did but never saw her actually do: Volunteer at the humane society. Serve dinner to the homeless. Run food and clothing drives. Use her celebrity status for endorsements and donations to worthy causes.

"And just like that, this beautiful child, this wonderful *spirit* has disappeared into thin air. At this point, the police are tight lipped, but there is one suspect."

I didn't realize I'd gasped until I heard it.

The next photo on the screen was me. It was grainy, a bad yearbook shot from last year. I was in the middle of a basketball game. It was the third quarter at least, and my hair was too long and shaggy. It hung in my eyes, and my lips were pursed into a weird, hard snarl. We were down by fourteen, I remembered weirdly. It was a tough game. I was playing on a sprained ankle. I looked like the dirty townie mechanic to the golden Hope in her glorious pigtails, holding out her dress and singing about rainbows and golden bricks.

Even I hated myself.

The news program dissolved into another shot, and I was mesmerized. It was the first time I met Hope's parents, the first time I was ever on TV, and I look dazed and drugged, wearing the blazer with shoulder pads that make me look half-linebacker, half-eighties-career-woman. I waved stupidly while the Jensens laughed, and although I knew the smile on Hope's face was painted on in front of gritted teeth, she looked perfect and normal.

The program went back to the hard-looking anchorwoman: "That is Hope's boyfriend—excuse me, ex-boyfriend—Tony Gardner. That was his first appearance on the *Wake Up the Bay!* show, his first introduction to the viewing world. According to police, Hope broke up with Tony just days before her disappearance. So the big question on everyone's mind is whether Tony had anything to do with Hope's disappearance. Jilted lover, or could it be something more? I mean, when this kid lost Hope, he also lost all this." The anchorwoman gestured over her shoulder to the picture still on the screen—me, Hope, and the Jensens, the three of them looking perfectly in their element, and me looking like a foster kid at his first feast. "Was it too much for Gardner?"

Bellingham paused the program and turned the screen back around. "See? They're trying to paint you as trailer trash who hooked himself to a lucky star. The thought is, Hope left you, and you couldn't—"

"I broke up with her," I corrected.

"Why?"

"It wasn't one thing. It was a lot of things. We're just really different. Different worlds, you know?"

"Yeah, I get it. I saw the report."

I swung my head. "That's not how it was at all. I didn't want any of that…Hope's fame or whatever. I mean, that segment there… I was duped. I didn't even know until I got there that it was going to be on TV. If anything, they were using me."

Bellingham was nodding with me, working his laced fingers over one another.

"You believe me, right?"

"Doesn't matter what I believe. It's what the jury believes."

My skin suddenly felt too tight, and it felt like my eyes were bulging out of my head. "The jury?"

"If this thing gets that far."

ELEVEN

High-profile. Famous. The beautiful, tragically missing Hope Jensen, the shifty Tony Gardner.

Hope sure had a perfect setup. Or Hope had me perfectly set up.

I didn't want to be famous. When I met Hope, I'd heard that her parents had some TV show and that some people thought she was some kind of a celebrity, but that had nothing to do with why I wanted to go out with her. I wanted to go out with her because she was cool, funny, and so pretty, and she actually had a brain.

And the whole celebrity thing? It was weird. No one cared who I was until I was with Hope. That was kind of amazing. When you go through three years of high school with barely anyone knowing your name, then suddenly everyone wants to know everything about you... Well, that's kind of cool. But now it was awful.

"I thought there were still some privacy laws," my father said while clucking his tongue at an article in the newspaper. "Aren't they not allowed to print his name because he's a minor?"

I shrugged. "Bellingham said I'm not a suspect. That because I haven't been charged with anything officially, they can say my name. Right to information or public record or something."

Hope must have known that. She must have known that she could up and disappear, and Renee and Ashleigh would let all the right people know that I was the last one to talk to Hope, the last one to argue with her—and they would come running: the police, the press.

I looked out the living room window, half expecting to see Bruce and Becky Jensen striding across our lawn, perfectly coifed, lapel mikes secure as they filmed a surprise-the-lowlife episode of *Wake Up the Bay!*

"I didn't do anything though. The only reason they're questioning me is because Hope was my girlfriend. And…I guess I was the last one to talk to her."

My mother smoothed her hands on her jeans. "I'm sure they're just trying to get all the information they can."

"Meanwhile, the media is dragging our son's name through the mud. There's got to be a law…" My dad was furious, pacing. I could tell it made my mother nervous, and I was glad that Alice was an iPad kid, completely absorbed in whatever cartoon was marching across the screen. "What did Mr. Bellingham say? There has to be something he can do."

I swallowed hard. "I just went to talk." My head started to swirl. Suspect. Attorneys. Missing kids, the media on my lawn, the police in my living room. If this *was* Hope, this was some evil plot.

Go big or go home, she always said.

I gritted my teeth. "It'll all blow over."

"How can you be so sure?" my mother asked.

I poured myself a glass of water and downed it. "I just know Hope."

Hope was going to pop out of the woodwork any day now, grinning—once she, the police, and the media had sufficiently pulverized me and my reputation—because that was the way Hope operated. That's what this was: a revenge plot. I had gotten one over on Hope, and she was going to tear me to shreds because of it.

I thought of the throbbing cursor urging me to share her location. I thought of myself typing *yes*.

Coincidence.

Hope was just trying to get back at me.

Right?

TWELVE
THE NIGHT SHE DISAPPEARED

Hope

The car tires squealed, and I flopped around in the backseat, arms crossed around my chest, legs pulled up in the fetal position, trying not to think of all the crap that had previously infected the blanket he draped over me. I had my hood zipped up to my chin, my hair tucked into a thick braid, and I kept my eyes clamped shut for the first twenty minutes of the ride.

I didn't speak to him; he didn't speak to me.

Rustin took a corner too sharply, and I slammed the top of my head against the car door.

"Can you take it easy, you freak?"

Rustin turned the music down, and I sat up, peering into the front seat. I caught his eyes in the rearview mirror. They were saucer wide, and there was a sheen of sweat over the few hairs on his upper lip.

"Sorry, I've never kidnapped anyone before. Can you keep your head down, please?"

Rustin was frustratingly basic at best, completely annoying at worst, but he was my best bet—my only bet, really. I sat up a little higher and cupped my hands around the window, peering into the darkness.

"Aren't we out of town yet?"

"Not quite. Like, five more minutes. Can you please just get down? If someone sees you, your flawless plan will be over."

I shrugged, let the blanket fall back to the floor, and stretched out across the backseat. "We're in the clear."

Rustin caught my eye in the rearview mirror. "You're supposed to have been kidnapped. Disappeared without a trace."

I unzipped my hoodie, shimmied out of that, and grinned when I noticed Rustin's gaze go low in the mirror to see my cleavage. I pushed it out a little bit. "We're fine. No one saw us." I pressed closer to the front seat. "No one saw us, right?"

Rustin wagged his head. "I kept a look out; you made the call."

"We are so not going to get caught. No one is even near our trail. I dumped my cell phone in the gutter at my place so…"

"So?"

"So, if I know Tony"—I rolled my eyes—"and I do know Tony, he'll have completely freaked out, tried to call me back. When I don't answer, he'll do the heroic thing and head to my house. No one will be there, but, shock of all shocks, he'll find the cell phone."

"If your cell phone is at your house, how did you call him?"

I wagged the brand-spanking-new phone in the palm of my hand. "Burner phone and an American Express black card."

"What if Tony goes to the police with your crushed cell phone?"

I waved my hand. "Tony won't do that. Not at first anyway. He'll wait to talk to my parents. Believe me, I know exactly what I'm doing."

Rustin cut his eyes to me, but he didn't look convinced. I wasn't exactly in the mood, but I played along. "If the police get involved, so what? I'll be famous."

"You're staging a kidnapping. Your own kidnapping. I'm pretty sure that's some sort of crime, like a felony or something."

I was getting annoyed. "And you're my accomplice, so you'd better keep your mouth shut, okay?"

Rustin was chewing the inside of his cheek. "You said this would just be a little prank to get back at Tony."

"It is."

"And if you get caught…"

That struck me, and my good humor died away, immediately replaced by a streak of anger. "*We're* not going to get caught. My plan is foolproof. And everyone will get what they deserve." I let my eyes trail down to Rustin, brushed my fingertips over his collarbone, and dipped my fingers into his shirt. His skin was soft, hot. I felt his pulse quicken, and that made me laugh too. I leaned closer and let the edges of my lips brush his ear. "Even you."

The car's speedometer went up ten miles.

"Get back there and lie down, please," Rustin told me, his voice even and tight.

I flipped back onto the seat, lay down, and giggled. "You're awfully fun to play with, Rustin."

He took another corner at top speed, and I careened across the backseat, now screaming and laughing. I rolled down the window and let the night air roll in, drinking it up. "This is fun!"

"I'm glad you think so." Rustin was not amused, but I didn't care.

Everything was falling into place.

* * *

Rustin's cabin wasn't the Four Seasons, but it wasn't totally terrible either. The furniture was old and unmatched, kind of mashed together with a funky, kitschy motel/trailer park vibe. At least it was pretty clean and there was a TV—and frankly, by the looks of the place, no one would think to look for me here.

I looked around, Rustin at my left shoulder. "It's nice."

"Just hang out, lie low. Don't make a mess or anything."

I flopped on the couch and kicked my feet up on the coffee table layered with dust. "How would anyone know if I did?"

Rustin didn't answer, and I blew out a sigh. "Everything will be great. Don't you worry."

I could see him shift his weight from foot to foot.

"You're not exactly doing this out of the goodness of your own heart, you know."

"What is that supposed to mean?"

I scooched forward on the old couch, a broken spring poking me in the thigh. "I have a plan that needs executing. You have a speeding ticket that will drain your bank account. I need a place to crash. You need almost a thousand dollars. You keep your mouth shut; I keep my mouth shut. I get my revenge on that idiot Tony, and you get to pay off your ticket with your parents never even knowing. See? Win, win."

Rustin still seemed anxious, but that went away once I put the money in his hands.

Boys were so easy.

Before he left, Rustin gave me two bags full of groceries—or what teenage boys assume pass for groceries—chips and sodas, beef jerky, cheese in a can, and a bag of baby carrots tossed in to make it girly, I guess.

I was eating the carrots while flipping channels on the TV. There was nothing on, but I keep checking the news incessantly to see if anything had come up about me yet. I knew it wouldn't tonight. Even if Tony did call the police, they wouldn't send out notices to the press yet. It'd be the basic "We'll do a welfare check," and they'd send a squad car to our place. But since Mom and Dad were such good parents, they wouldn't be home, instead donating their cheesy, white smiles and perky television personae to an auction benefitting someone else's children—fosters or adoptees or amputees or something. The police would knock on the front door, look through the windows, and eventually give up.

I watched as Rustin's taillights disappeared down the dirt road in front of the house. There was the groan of the engine, the ping of gravel against the back fenders of the car, and then...nothing. The stillness was complete, the silence deafening and odd. I was used to nominal noise even in our place, which is set away in the back of the neighborhood. There was always a leaf blower roaring or a car screaming down the highway behind us. Either way, there also was always at least one television on and one radio or Internet connection autoplaying some stupid commercial in the house. But out here in the woods, in the middle of nowhere, there was nothing. No low electric drone. No hum of streetlights. I sighed, and the sound reverberated back to me. Once Rustin's headlights finished snaking their way down the long drive and hit that left turn onto the main road, there was darkness too.

Complete. Engulfing.

I took a few steps outside, admiring the burst of stars overhead. When the breeze kicked up, I could hear the rustle of the pines all around me. Although the sound should have been nature-y and comforting, all I could think of was being on the set of my parents' show, the rustle of people pushing past with earpieces or racks of costumes or stopping to snap pictures of everything, mimicking the shooshing sound of the trees.

I wondered what my parents were doing right then.

Bruce and Becky Jensen, the darlings of Channel 7's *Wake Up the Bay!* They were perfect people living perfect lives as perfectly coifed coanchors who fell in love on the job—or so the story goes. They had never wanted children, based on the assumption that kids would affect their upward media mobility, but my mom's unexpected pregnancy—and her hard-hitting, tear-jerking, *it-happened-to-me* story on her subsequent miscarriage—vaulted them from a half-hour spot at 5:00 a.m. to a full-hour talk show format at 9:00 a.m. Thus, she immediately set to work getting knocked up with me, and their ratings soared.

I became the perfect poster child, the puppy that stole the show, and every aspect of my gestation to birth was broadcast live (or very close to it). Even my name was a media stunt. I was dubbed Hope Adelaide Jensen, not because it bore any family history or deep sentimental meaning to either of my parents, but because that was what a bunch of bacon-breathed morning television watchers voted to name me.

My mom and I were both showered with flowers, balloons, and gifts from strangers when I was born, and I still got the occasional cheap stuffed bear or balloon-o-gram from Celia in Pittsburgh or Phil in the South Bay. It was weird and unnerving, but my parents always pulled the trinket onto the show and fell all over themselves thanking their viewing family for keeping their precious baby girl in their thoughts. Sometimes they'd bring the gift home for me, but more often than not, it went to the cameraman or the craft services person as further proof that my parents were the best, most unselfish television personalities ever.

But for all their focus-on-the-family segments spotlighting the best birthday parties, family harmony, and sing-along road trips, Bruce and Becky were shitty parents. They'd missed almost every one of my birthdays because my birthday generally falls around Oscar Sunday, when my parents spend the week reporting from the Beverly Hills Hotel. They told me it was not a big deal because they always threw a huge on-air birthday bash for me two weeks later in March during the ratings slump.

They'd trot me out, and my mother would tearfully recount how it had been a sunny day when I made my way into the world and the television viewers' hearts. (It was a rainy day in February, and my mother demanded a C-section and a plastic surgeon.) There were more gifts from complete strangers and cutaways to actual celebrities who have actual March birthdays. The event culminated with a cardboard birthday cake with sparklers and the studio audience clapping maniacally as if they'd never before been offered a slice of grocery birthday cake on a paper plate. The audience whooped when they got goodie bags, and I got driven back to school in a town car.

So really, this whole thing was going to be good for my parents.

Standing there outside the cabin, I almost got a sense of something—guilt or regret—but it was quickly stamped out by the memory of an afternoon a few days ago when I let myself in from school. There was a *shoosh-shoosh* sound as a woman I'd never seen before pushed a rack full of evening gowns wrapped in plastic down our hallway, and another woman guarded the door to my mother's bedroom.

"Becky can't see you right now, honey," this strange woman said to me. "We're getting ready for the banquet tonight."

"It's okay," I heard Mom yell. "It's just Hope."

I shimmied by the woman with the dresses. My mother was seated at her dressing room table being fawned and fussed over by half the staff from the morning show and a half-dozen other people I've never seen before. They were prepping her with brushes and shooting her with hair spray. Mom poked out a perfectly manicured hand and waved.

"Hi." I waved back, stupidly.

"School okay?"

I wanted to tell her what had been happening, that I kind of missed Tony, but she didn't make eye contact with me or expect me to answer her. Her hand disappeared back into the crush of people. Someone was layering her wrists with glittering bracelets, and someone else was telling her to "close, pucker, kiss," while they slathered her with another layer of makeup. There was a sliver of room where I could see my mother in profile, but another woman came in and fit herself in that space, and I had to step back because I was in the way. Someone from the production team stepped forward with a clipboard, and I have to take another step back.

Someone else counted down the time. A man with three shoe boxes shoved me aside, and suddenly I was standing in the hallway, watching my mom get smaller and farther away, less and less interested in me or anything I had to say.

A rustling in the trees snapped me back to night outside the cabin, and I sighed, stepped back in the house, and slammed the door behind me.

I'd be lucky if my parents noticed I was gone at all.

And then there was Tony.

I flicked a few more channels and crunched down on a handful of baby carrots.

I had really loved Tony. Or, whatever passes for love in messed-up high school meets television-celebrity land. He wasn't a jock or a nerd or really any kind of standout guy, which is what I really liked about him—and what ended up ruining everything.

We were in Mr. Abel's chemistry class—a class I deplored. Mr. A was having some sort of conniption (again), handing out test papers because most of the class had failed. He was going on and on about *this generation* and how we weren't applying ourselves and had no attention span other than our phones or something stupid like that. No one was listening because he had these fits all the time, and if he were a better teacher, maybe more of us would pass, right?

Anyway, Mr. A's answer to his own bad teaching was to make a new seating chart. I guess he thought if we weren't sitting next to someone interesting, he could be the most interesting thing in the room (uh, never). So, Tony and I got seated next to each other. I could see from his test paper that he got a B+, but he kind of shuffled his paper like it was no big deal. I got an A–. I pretty much always got A's.

Some of the other guys started making jokes, making fun of Mr. A. Look, I don't like the guy, but I really hated when these idiots went off—their humor was so *juvenile*. Then Mr. A stopped his rant for, like, a minute and got all red faced, and the hyenas in the back row started laughing like they'd actually made a real funny. It made me feel bad for Mr. Abel. He was just doing his best, I guessed, and having spent actual time with Jimmy Nugent and Tommy Cox, I knew they were complete toolbox assholes who had been telling the same jokes since the third grade.

Back to Tony.

So, everyone laughs when Jimmy and Tommy laugh because they're high up on the Florence High food chain, and frankly, no one wanted to be the butt of their next stupid joke. I didn't care; I didn't laugh.

Neither did Tony.

He glanced at me and shook his head, rolling those eyes that I had never noticed were the exact shade of sky blue I wanted to paint everything in my life. He muttered something under his breath, and I leaned in, suddenly desperate to hear his voice, but the first thing I noticed was the way that he smelled: like soap. Not some fancy, stupid body spray from one of those commercials where girls stick to shirtless guys, but just…soap. Basic. Simple. You could tell the scent was something with a real name like *cotton* or *linen* and not *urban jungle* or *Biscayne breeze*.

"What did you say?"

Tony's eyes flashed this awesome streak of blue that shot through me like a lightning bolt. "I said, of all people, those idiots should pay attention in this class. You know they're going to blow up their meth lab two months after we graduate."

And get this: I giggled. *I giggled*. Like, a high-pitched, stupid girl giggle even though I didn't really get his joke.

First of all, I wasn't that kind of girl. I didn't date high school guys, because they were idiots who dared each other to eat things for a dollar, and I had bigger and better things going on in my life. Besides, most of the guys around here grew up here, went to school here, got fat and bald here, then died here. I planned on getting out of here the second after I grabbed my diploma, and I wasn't taking any high school baggage with me.

But Tony…

So I was lost in his eyes. And his scent. And then I giggled. And then…he ignored me. Not ignored me, ignored me, but usually most guys fall for me. I'm pretty and I'm super popular, which is why I hate most of the guys that fall into my lap. They want to do things for me, and within a week, they're falling all over me—and we all know it's because I'm popular and have great tits. But Tony didn't say much more to me that day, and the next day, I asked him if he wanted me to help him study for the next quiz.

He didn't.

He had some dumb excuse like his little sister or something, and once again, he smelled *so good* and his eyes were so bright, and when he smiled, he had this one little dimple that looked so totally out of place but so cute. We talked about nothing until Mr. A told us to be quiet. Then, get this, Tony *blushed*! Like, an actual full-on, red-cheeked blush, and I had to make him my project right then and there. He wasn't popular. He wasn't even considered cute. But what really mattered was that he didn't seem to care who I was.

He didn't say a thing about my parents or even sputter that he watched them before school or that his parents DVR'd them or whatever. He didn't ask what it was like to live in a mansion or if I really have two full-time maids, or stare at my chest when he talked. He just looked me in the eye and talked. And when I said Death to Sea Monkeys was also my favorite band, he burned me a copy of their bootleg album, even though I'd had it for weeks because they were on my parents' show. He just thought I was a regular girl. And he was a regular guy.

He *was*.

We were dating for about three months before my parents met him. By that time, I had met his parents and his baby sister (who really was kind of a doll). His whole family was regular and cool, and they had dinner at six o'clock every day when his dad came home from work and hung up his jacket and actually kissed his mom. Sometimes he would even slap her on the butt and Tony would shake his head, but I thought it was supercute.

I could imagine me and Tony living like that one day, maybe, in a little townie house that could use a full upgrade but we would be happy, and we would still have the long, intense conversations that we had every day—travel, politics, the state of the world, animal welfare. We talked about stuff that mattered, while every other couple in our school talked about prom and who did what with whom and who would do even more. Sure, I still intended to go to college and travel and be successful and make my mark on the world, but being with Tony made being a townie wife seem so nice and comfortable and…happy.

And then Tony met my parents.

It was a setup, of course: brunch at our country club. My mother came by my room before we left to check my outfit. I should have known then that she had something up her sleeve. Whenever she checks that the whole family wears the same color palette, we end up with an "impromptu" photo opportunity, or a camera crew just happens to be in the corner under some fake fern. Both my parents would act like they didn't see Ted and Juan and Mowgli—the show's camera guy, boom operator, and key grip—even through Ted is the size of a minivan, Juan has been to every family event since my birth, and Mowgli has a mouth full of gold teeth that make him look like a Vegas jack-o'-lantern.

I should have known when Tony walked in looking completely dazed. His dark, floppy curls were slicked back, and he was wearing a stiff, brand-new-looking navy blazer over his well-worn khakis. When he waved at me—a weird, mechanical wave—I knew that someone had prepped him, told him he would be on camera, and when I saw the little purple tag pop out of his shirt-sleeve, I knew that his outfit had been commandeered from the wardrobe department.

Then, of course, Mom and Dad grinned their perfect smiles of Chiclet teeth and addressed Tony and then an imaginary studio audience, and I knew *Wake Up the Bay!* was filming another Hope Life Event. I wanted to stab Tony in the eye and murder my parents right then and there—because what normal girl introduces her first serious boyfriend to her parents and the American viewing public at the same time? Of course my mother would never tell me ahead of time, because then she wouldn't get the Real Teenage Reaction that the fans so counted on.

Tony swore up and down that he drove to the country club and was immediately pulled aside by someone in a hot-pink pantsuit— Betty Sue Luellen, the woman with three first names who produced *Wake Up the Bay!*—and was escorted into the coatroom where he was handed a new shirt and the blazer before someone globbed a handful of something shiny and sticky in his hair. He was told that I knew about the show and to "act natural."

I *didn't* know... And natural? Tony looked like a deer in headlights the whole time, but my parents, consummate professionals, made big, grand jokes that the producers attached a laugh track to in post-production and cut away in between courses for words from our sponsors. Those cutaways were the most awkward—Tony tried to keep up with my parents' vague questions, while two women with powder puffs and tiny brushes touched up my parents' perfect faces. Finally, Tony took my hand under the table and whispered, "The show is only an hour long, right?"

I nodded, and when the conversation died down and the last course was finished and the sponsors thanked, Tony asked if he could drive me home after we took a walk. My parents agreed, and we drove to the beach, laughing at my parents and my stupid life the whole time. I laughed so hard tears rolled down my face, and then Tony pulled off the highway and looked hard at me, his fingers against my chin.

I stopped laughing, but I couldn't stop crying because this was my life—fake even when I implored it to be real. Tony kissed me hard and long, and after a while, he broke away from me and looked at me with those deep-cobalt eyes once again and said, "I *see you*, Hope. I want you to know that."

I had been looked at my whole life—on TV, in the newspaper, at school—but Tony Gardner was the first person that actually *saw* me. At least I thought he did. And then he ruined it. And now he had to pay.

THIRTEEN
TWO DAYS MISSING

Hope

"Hope, Hope, Hope…"

My mother's voice was strong, then trailed off, strangled in a bunch of voices I didn't recognize. Then, my father: "We're waiting for you, Hope. We just want you to come home safely."

I sat up and blinked, looking around. There was a filtered gray haze in the house, and my eyes flitted around the room: Ugly plaid couch. Rocking chair with all the pillows smashed down. Faded curtains. Where—

Rustin's cabin.

I flopped onto the floor and stared at the TV, rubbing my eyes with the backs of my hands. Mom and Dad's *Wake Up the Bay!* show. Same logos, same text, different background.

Home.

Mom and Dad were sitting in our "formal" living room, perched on the white couch that no one has ever sat on, the enormous family picture of the three of us just visible over Dad's left-hand shoulder in the shot. Mom was carrying a picture of me in a massive wooden frame. My mother was quiet, playing the part of the wounded matriarch with Oscar-worthy grace. Her cheeks, eyes, and nose were the requisite pink, but not red enough to be ugly. She dabbed gently at her eyes with an embroidered handkerchief I didn't know she owned. My father looked resplendent in a suit I'm pretty sure he wore to the Emmys, but his lapel was comfortably crushed, his white shirt rumpled enough to be relatable because no one irons through grief.

"Hope is our world," my father was saying. "She's everything to us. We prayed every day to have a baby before she was born…"

I snorted.

I was a ratings boost.

There was a newscaster sitting opposite my aggrieved parents. I recognized him from a national syndicate and wondered how my parents were keeping their excitement in check.

Consummate professionals.

"Mr. and Mrs. Jensen, can you please tell us exactly what transpired the night that Hope went missing?" The lines of the newscaster's suit were as rigid as his over-gelled hairstyle. He had the practiced, professionally earnest look of a journalist who had wormed his way into television and viewers' hearts with human-interest stories, and my parents were playing right into his hands—and he into theirs.

My mother looked piteous and put a hand on my father's, giving a gentle squeeze. My father sucked in a deep, steadying breath, and I wanted to puke.

"Well, Becky and I were hosting a benefit for the new pediatric wing of the children's hospital that night. We had left Hope in the early evening."

I wanted to scream. They walked out. Didn't say good-bye. Didn't offer me the obligatory twenty bucks for takeout or mention a frozen pizza for dinner. We were beyond that as a family. We were three people living in a house, living separate lives strung together with film footage. I groaned and rolled my eyes.

"We were home not long past eleven, and when my wife"—here they shared a meaningful glance—"went in to check on Hope, she wasn't in her bed."

A single tear made its way down my mother's cheek, her nostrils daintily flaring.

"We called Hope's cell phone, looked at her social media, checked with her friends…"

I glanced at my phone and saw that my parents had indeed called me—at ten o'clock the following morning. They had access to my public social media accounts because those had been set up and were carefully cultivated by *Wake Up the Bay!* Basically, a litany of good kid doing good-kid thing posts: "Mall with my besties!" "At the big game!"

Good, diligent parenting, Bruce and Becky.

"We called the police."

"And the police responded right away? Usually, we know that it takes a minimum of twenty-four hours for law enforcement to move on a missing persons case. Particularly when it involves a teenager." The newscaster takes turns looking from my parents to the camera.

My mother looked sheepish, and my father let her talk. "We called a family friend who is a member of the police force. He's known Hope her whole life. Knows—as we do—that Hope is a good girl. She's not one to wander off or go off with friends without letting us know."

I laughed, rooted through the paper grocery bag that Rustin had left, and popped the top on a tube of Sour Cream and Onion Pringles. Usually, I don't eat crap like that, but my parents' current performance had rendered everything ridiculous.

My mother's eyes were huge, wide, and crystal blue like mine, and even though they were rimmed with manufactured tears, her mascara didn't dare smudge. "He came over right away and took our statement. By the next morning, the police were mobilized, ready to look for...for—" A sob, a perfectly manicured hand splayed against her chest, a wide shot going in for a tighter angle on my mom's anguished face—"for my baby."

I couldn't take it anymore. I flipped a few channels. Every other one was the same shot, the same living room arrangement: tortured mother, anguished father, practiced news anchor. I had a vague sense of satisfaction and pride. Things were working out better than I had expected—almost. My parents' reaction was basically textbook. I had expected the fake anguish, the special report from the formal living room, but the national news anchor was a nice touch.

I found some rerun of a rerun and kicked my shoes off, cuddling up on the couch and going through a quarter sleeve of Pringles—they really weren't half-bad—when the show was broken into with a surge of percussive music and another coifed but stern-looking anchor. I was about to change the channel when the image of my parents was changed to a live action shot of a woman standing in front of my high school. I leaned forward and clicked the volume up.

"Thanks, Stan. I'm here at Florence High School, which missing student Hope Jensen normally attends. As you can see here, the student body is quite concerned…"

The cameraman did a panning shot of the front of the school where kids were milling about, a few in huddles. I smiled when he slowly panned over a length of hurricane fence that my classmates had decorated with teddy bears, flowers, and a huge, glitter-bordered picture of me. People I didn't recognize were leaning down lighting candles, and several that I do know were hugging and crying, shying away from the camera. The scene was so somber and sad that I wanted to reach out and let my friends in on the joke—but it was touching too, and I loved what they'd done. I'd only been gone a day and a half, and already I was immortalized.

FOURTEEN

Tony

She'd already been immortalized. Teddy bears and flowers wrapped in tissue and cellophane littered the sidewalk along the school fence. There were candles and sniffling students and a larger-than-life-size picture of Hope, grinning, that someone had glued gold glitter all around. I wondered where they got all this stuff—and how, since the news had barely broken. Was there some twenty-four-hour news-tragedy pop-up kiosk or something?

I shuffled through and tried to keep my head down, but people were already looking at me, giving me sidelong glances, whispering. "Hope has been kidnapped," "What if she's dead?" "Do you think Tony had something to do with it?"

I tried to ignore them, tried not to think about Hope.

What if…? I wouldn't let myself think about it. Hope was fine. Hope was strong and sharp, and even if someone did take her…

My stomach clenched, and I could feel a slight headache licking at my temples.

"There he is! He's right there!"

I whirled around because I recognized the voice—Everly Byer, one of Hope's frenemies. When I looked, she was pointing right at me, pointing me out to a woman in a suit. I wondered if the woman was CIA or FBI until she came pounding toward me, microphone clutched in her hand. Someone stopped her, and I used the opportunity to disappear into the crowd, slipping into the school.

I made a beeline for the computer lab. The Jensen Computer Lab, donated by Hope's folks. There was an autographed black-and-white framed photo of them on the wall. I ignored it, feeling a pang of guilt as I did so.

I stayed in the computer lab until people started flooding the library. At first I thought it was just a normal class, a normal rush of students, but then I saw the camera people, an anchor I recognized from *Wake Up the Bay!*, the makeup lady with her giant black makeup box, and the boom operators with fluffy mikes and stadium lights. I stared, transfixed, as two guys carried away a display of "Hot Teen Reads" and replaced it with a potted plant and a couple of chairs.

"Total zoo."

Some kid I didn't recognize came into the computer lab and took one of the chairs in the darkened room. He was shaking his head, about to replace his earbuds when I stopped him.

"What's all this about?"

"That missing chick, Hope something or other?"

My stomach twisted and I tried to gulp, hoping I don't look as stupidly terrified as I felt. "Jensen," I said quietly.

"Yeah. News reporters or whatever are interviewing students."

"What about the police?"

The kid shrugged and folded a piece of gum into his mouth. "They're all over the place too. Why do you think I'm holed up in here?" His grin made me uneasy. "Am I right?"

"I'm just…" My eyes drifted to my open screen, to the message still awaiting Hope's response. I clicked it off. "Doing homework. So this is the news? Are they taking statements?"

Again the kid shrugged. "I'm kind of new here. Naz." He didn't hold out a hand or wave or anything, then went on talking. "Not like this at my old school." He looked around and kind of grinned. "Better computer lab here though." He yanked a nice-looking machine out of his bag and set up at one of the laptop stations. "Kind of my thing."

"Oh. So, you don't know what they're really doing out there?"

Naz was obviously starting to lose interest in the conversation. "They're just asking for people who want to"—and here he made air quotes—"'express their sentiments' for the missing chick."

"Hope."

"Huh?"

I let out a breath. "Her name is Hope."

"Whatever. She's probably holed up in some hotel room with some dude or, I don't know, in, like, Rio or something."

I straightened. "Why do you say that?"

"Rich bitch, right? That's what I heard. If I were her, I would have blown this shit school and shit town ages ago. Who are you again?"

I turned the computer off completely. "No one."

All heads snapped toward me when I stepped out of the computer lab and the door slammed shut behind me.

"That's the ex-boyfriend!" I heard.

I craned and could see that Everly was pointing me out again. The news anchor sprang from her makeup chair, wearing a bib made out of Kleenex. She speed walked toward me.

"Tony, Tony Gardner, right? We'd really love to get a statement from you." She sort of shook her head and wiggled her butt when she asked me, a big, greasy smile spread across her face. There was lipstick on her teeth.

"No thank you." I turned, but she grabbed my arm, her painted nails talon-like, her grip firmer than I expected.

"But it's for Hope."

That gave me pause. "How so?"

"We're making a tribute to her. For her." The anchorwoman cocked her head and offered another smile, this one a combination of the previous lipstick-toothed radiance and something I assumed was supposed to be sincerity.

"How is this going to help find Hope?"

"Well, maybe she'll see it and know how much we all miss her. How all of you have come together"—she made a sweeping gesture with her arm—"to support her."

"Wouldn't it make more sense to be out looking for her?"

The smile dropped from the anchorwoman's lips. "Are you going to participate or not? Frankly, I would if I were you. It'll look better."

"What does that mean? 'It'll look better'?"

Now I'd annoyed the anchorwoman. She dropped her whole charm act, blew out a curt sigh, and popped her hip. "We both know Hope didn't just go missing, Tony." Her gaze was simmering, fixed on mine, and it was unnerving. I tried to keep my cool.

"We do?"

"Stranger kidnappings rarely happen. A teen being killed by a jealous ex?" She looked me up and down, and I took a step back.

"I've got to go."

"Your funeral," I heard her call behind me.

I slowed down but didn't turn around. There was a flurry of activity behind me, and when I finally did turn, I noticed the anchorwoman had pulled off the Kleenex bib, had been fitted with a microphone, and was bathed in fake yellow television light.

"Is there anything you would like to tell Hope?" she asked after me, her voice a smooth, soothing octave I recognized immediately from television.

There were two cameras on me. Four lights. A sea of faces staring, dead silent, interested. I was sweating, but I couldn't tell if it was from the lights or the rage generated by this fucking "Tribute to Hope."

"I would tell Hope that I won't stop looking for her. That if I were her parents…" I looked around the makeshift set at the stupid potted plants and plastic chairs. "If I were her parents and had the money and resources they have, I wouldn't waste them on publicity or flowers or stupid tribute shows. I would find her."

The library was silent when I slammed the door behind me.

* * *

There were fewer reporters on the lawn when I got home. Two, maybe three—definitely a lady chain-smoking near my mom's azalea bushes and a guy in a half-unbuttoned shirt who held a Styrofoam coffee cup to his lips while he stared me down. He took a sip from the cup and started *chewing*. If my stomach weren't already in one giant snarl, I might have thrown up. Neither of them made a move toward me. Neither did either of the people in the news van with one open door and the whirl of machines working inside. I guess we were just supposed to ignore each other.

When I got inside the house, it was dim and cool from the curtains being drawn. Mom and Dad were home and sitting on the couch. They were watching TV but turned it off the second I walked in the door.

"Hey, guys."

They took a moment to compose themselves or something, and Alice used that same moment to run in and throw her arms around me. She had some Disney doll in her hands with a big plastic head that thunked against the back of my legs while she squeezed.

"Hey, squirt."

"Hey, squirt," she parroted back. "You're famous!"

"Alice, stop." My mom stood up, walked around the couch, and pried Alice from my legs. "Go get yourself something to eat."

"I'm not hungry."

"Then go get Tony something to eat."

I raised my eyebrows. "I'm famous?"

It was my father's turn to stand now, to come around the

THE REVENGE

couch and fix me with eyes that all at once looked a hundred years older than they had this morning and like he hadn't slept in, well, ever.

"You're all over the news, Tony."

I felt myself pale, even though I wasn't surprised.

My mom's eyes were glassy, and the idea that she was about to cry twisted something tight and painful in my gut.

"What's going on, Tony? What are you involved with?"

"Nothing, Ma—"

"Don't shut us out!" My dad's voice was firm but tinged with exhaustion and…despair?

I raked my hands through my hair, paced, and ended up on the couch. "The police…everyone…seems to think I know where Hope is. Or that I had something to do with her disappearance."

My mother crossed her arms in front of her chest, rubbing her elbows like the temperature had suddenly dropped ten degrees. It hadn't. I picked at my collar. If anything, it was about ten degrees hotter than five minutes ago.

"We don't believe you have anything to do with this."

I should have felt relieved—elated, even—but guilt sat like a big, black rock in my gut.

The guilt was immediately eaten away by defensiveness.

Hope's mocking sneer… Her spiderlike fingers as she plucked open that stupid paper, that stupid poem, then pursed her lips… Her voice cotton-candy sweet at first, then cloying, choking… "Our love is a flower that blooms…"

The raucous sound of laughter thundered through my head.

93

Share Location?

The throbbing cursor...

* * *

I didn't know what time my parents went to bed, but Alice was snoring in her room and I was staring at my bedroom ceiling when I heard the first tiny rasp against my window. I assumed that first one was the wind pushing something against the glass, but then it stopped and started again, a little more insistent. I tried to ignore it, because if it wasn't the bushes, it was probably one of the reporters—the coffee-chewing guy or the chain-smoking woman—but when I'd glanced out the window before bed, they were suddenly friends and crawling into the same gold-colored Dodge something or other.

Another scratch, then this time a...knock?

I rolled out of bed and crouched down, sweat breaking out at my hairline.

It was Hope.

It had to be.

Another sound, like pebbles on the window.

Definitely Hope.

My heart thudded, and I couldn't tell if I was smiling or grimacing. I wanted her home. I wanted her back so she could be out of my life legitimately and for good. I wanted her home so that I knew she was safe.

I pushed open the window, and a whoosh of air came in, tinged with the same bright jasmine smell that wafted from Hope every time she moved her hair. She was outlined in the moonlight, though half shadowed by bushes.

"I didn't think you were going to open the window."

Not Hope. Everly Byer. One of Hope's early henchwomen.

"What are you doing here?"

Everly crossed her arms in front of her chest and did a Hope-esque almost-pout. "Aren't you going to let me in?"

I looked down at the window. "Come around back."

I was padding to the sliding glass door, but I didn't know what I was doing. Why would Everly show up at my house? When I stepped into the kitchen, she was at the back door, dressed in a plaid skirt and some kind of leggings or tights with a jean jacket, and her hair curled all around her shoulders. At a glance and standing there in the faint moonlight, she almost looked like Hope. I didn't know much about Everly, but I didn't remember her being such a Hope clone.

When I slid open the door, she stepped in without being asked, rubbing her hands along her arms like it was freezing out. I poked my head out into the darkness; it was warm.

"What are you doing here, Everly?"

"Hello to you too."

I sighed. "It's the middle of the night."

"It's ten forty-five."

"Not exactly visiting hours."

Everly sat at my kitchen table. "Well, I couldn't just pop in during the day, now could I? Can I get a glass of water?"

I didn't know why, but I opened the fridge and poured us two glasses, then sat across from her. She took a sip of her water and held it in her mouth, her eyes flitting all over the kitchen. "Nice place."

I pinned her with a glare.

She sighed. "Let me start over. Hey, Tony."

"Hey, Everly. What are you doing here?"

She sucked in a low breath as if she was deciding whether to tell me the truth.

"Are you doing okay?" she asked finally.

I was caught off guard and chugged my whole glass of water. "Uh…"

Everly reached out a hand and clasped mine so they were both wrapped around the glass. "I don't believe what they're saying about you."

"What who is saying?"

"Everyone. At school, the media, the cops."

I didn't know why I bothered to ask.

"I don't think you hurt Hope, Tony. Actually…" She took her hands back, clasped them in front of her on the table, and shook her head, her blond curls rolling, the scent of jasmine shampoo wafting up. "I know you didn't."

My blood pressure started to ratchet up, and I sat closer. "Do you know where Hope is?"

She cocked her head, biting on her bottom lip. She wore the same shade of lipstick as Hope, but it looked odd on her, unnatural. On Hope, it blended seamlessly with her full, already red-pink lips.

"Not exactly. It's more like—" Everly paused to brush her hair over her shoulders. "I know you're not that kind of guy."

"Not what kind of guy?"

"The kind who would do something horrible to a girl." She blinked her eyes, and I noticed her lashes were long and too black. They got caught up in her bangs. "You're a good guy, Tony, and I want to help you. I know you didn't have anything to do with Hope's disappearance."

"Because I'm a good guy?"

She nodded slowly, her eyes locked on mine. "And I know how Hope can be."

I blinked. "You do?"

Everly stood and put her back to me like she was about to recite a monologue in some overdramatic movie. "You know we were best friends, right? Hope and me?"

I didn't, but I nodded anyway.

"In junior high and most of freshman year. You know she didn't even want to have anything to do with the show, right?"

I shrugged. "I guess."

"I mean, she does a little more now, but when it first started… nothing." Everly turned, shaking her head vehemently. "Her parents were constantly asking her to do things…little things, like a dance or just a segment. Once they asked us to do a fashion show before school started, but Hope didn't want to do it. She was stubborn."

I picked at a piece of rice stuck to the tabletop. "I don't know what any of this has to do with…"

"Hope always got her way. Always. But she listened to me for a little bit. We did the fashion show, and her parents loved it. The ratings went nuts, I guess. We made cookies on the Christmas special." Everly smiled, remembering. "Basically, we made a big mess with tons of red and green frosting, but everyone loved us. They thought we were so cute." She shrugged. "But I wasn't the Jensens' daughter. Hope was."

I stared at my hands and shook my head. "So?"

"So Hope started doing more things for the show…"

"And people started loving her."

Everly's eyes flashed. A muscle along her jawline flicked, and I could see that she was clenching her teeth. "Everyone. They were always praising her, giving her stuff."

I was getting tired. I yawned. "And?"

"And she ate it up. She didn't even want to do any of that stuff. She wouldn't have if it weren't for me." Everly's lips were set hard now, her hands were on her hips. "She wasn't into any of this."

"Until you convinced her."

"And then it became her way of life."

I showed Everly the palms of my hands, still confused. "So?"

"So? Don't you see? She's *still* doing it."

I sat up a little straighter. "What are you talking about, Everly? Do you know something? Did Hope tell you something?"

Everly sat down again, hard. Her eyes were still fixed, too bright; her irises were almost liquid. "I want to know what you know. Do you believe Hope is in any real danger, Tony?"

I bit my thumbnail. I stood and started to pace, while Everly sat quietly at my kitchen table, taking tiny sips from her water glass.

"I know it was you who put all her information online."

I stopped pacing but didn't look at Everly. "You do?"

She blew out an exasperated sigh. "Everyone does, Tony. It was actually pretty funny. Good prank."

I wondered if Everly had any idea how far it had gone.

"It was obvious how much it pissed Hope off." Everly's smile was wide, dazzling. She truly enjoyed Hope's annoyance. "And if I know Hope, you getting one over on her must have really pissed her off. She's the top dog, you know? At least she thinks she is. So…she needed to retaliate."

"What are you saying?"

She shrugged, looking completely nonchalant, like my life wasn't hanging in the balance. "I think she's probably in on this. You can't tell me you didn't have the same thought. I mean, I know you loved her and everything, but you can't be that dumb. She didn't love you. She doesn't. She doesn't love anyone. What she loves is having the last laugh."

I had been telling myself the same thing for days, but coming from Everly, it stung worse than it should have.

"So you want to find her…why?"

Everly crossed her arms and cocked a single brow. "I don't necessarily want to find her. I want to expose her." Just as quickly as that brow went up, it dropped back down, and her lower lip pushed out. "For you. I think what she did to you is awful."

I stopped pacing when Everly stood.

"You're too good for her, Tony. You always were. And this… You deserve to be happy. I want that for you."

She stepped closer to me, and suddenly, the walls of the kitchen bowed in and she was too close to me, the whole situation too tight. Everly leaned against me and used a single finger to trace the collar of my T-shirt. "I want to help you. I want to make things better for you. That's all I was... That's all I am trying to do."

Before I realized it, she was on her tiptoes, one hand splayed against my chest, the other tangled in the hair at the back of my head. Her lips were against mine, soft, then a little more insistent.

I was too stunned to kiss her back.

"Tony?"

It was Alice, in the doorway, sleepy-eyed and tousle-haired. She was wearing one of my basketball camp T-shirts as a nightgown, and it nearly reached her ankles.

"Is that Hope?"

Everly whirled as if she'd been electrocuted. "I'm not Hope."

Alice rubbed her eyes, edged past Everly, and opened the refrigerator. "Can I have milk?"

I took the carton from Alice and poured a half glass into her *Frozen* mug. "Yeah, but take it back to your room with you, okay, squirt?"

Still half asleep, Alice took the cup in both hands and drank a large slug. "Okay, squirt. Good night, Tony. Good night, Hope."

I watched her pad across the kitchen floor, bare feet making little *puff-puff* sounds. When I turned around, Everly was gone, the sliding door standing open, the cold night air wafting in.

I wanted to go back to sleep, but my whole body felt on edge, on fire. My heart was thrumming, blood rushed in my ears, and every time I tried to close my eyes, there was Hope, her sweet smile turning into a slow sneer. Then there was Everly with her lips pressed against mine, then snapping back like a coiled snake, when Alice called her Hope. I paced the house in the darkness, but the walls seemed to be vibrating, closing in.

I tried to watch TV, but every channel was a magic something-or-other: pan or weight-loss pill or cream, and every other channel was a rerun of the local news, with photographs of local events that always cycled back to Hope, back to the picture of her grinning, head thrown back, her teeth perfect and straight and even, her eyes boring into you, daring you to try to look away.

A lump burned in my throat every time I saw that picture, and I didn't know if I wanted to cry or scream. I hated her for being gone. I hated her for making me wonder. But somewhere, deep in my gut, I wanted her to be okay more than anything else. Not just because I wanted the cops to stop buzzing around me, wanted the press to get off my lawn, but because she was Hope and I did love her and I didn't want anything bad to…

I tossed the TV remote and went to my bedroom, firing up the laptop and pulling down my search history. I clicked on the oldest entry, the first site, the first time I exposed Hope to the world. My laptop whirred as the site popped up on-screen.

Hello, and welcome back Revenge723! You have 42 new messages.

My stomach clenched. I needed to delete my search history. I need to deactivate and delete this account.

You have 42 new messages.

I should check them. For Hope. I should check them because one of these messages could be the person who took her.

"No one took Hope," I muttered to myself, biting the inside of my cheek. "She did this… She's bluffing."

Everly's kiss burned against my lips. She seemed so sure…

I clicked the first message.

From JONNY61: UR gorgeous. Cant believe someone who looks like U doesn't have a boyfriend.

From JSHADE: You're like 5 miles from me. Wanna get together?

I blinked and clicked through several more messages. Most mimicked the first two: *You're pretty, can't believe you don't have a boyfriend, want to meet up?* I was about to click off when one message caught my eye.

RIDETHEWAVE: I know you.

I read the sentence, three stupid words, and ice water shot through my veins. Totally benign. Nonthreatening. It wouldn't be odd for someone to know Hope, especially someone local or even someone in the state. The Jensens' show was syndicated. Portions of the program had been shown on the occasional national news channels. The daily show streamed online and plastered billboards, web pages, and commercials with ads, most of them just showing Bruce and Becky, but more than occasionally showing Hope too.

I intended to delete the account. I intended not to look back. But Ridethewave's next post caught my eye.

RIDETHEWAVE: Got you in my sights.

"No big deal," I mumbled.

RIDETHEWAVE: Locked and loaded.

My stomach roiled, and the ice water that shot through my veins turned into a white-hot heat, a deep, dark pit in my gut.

RIDETHEWAVE: Gotcha.

FIFTEEN
THREE DAYS MISSING

Hope

I clicked on Rustin's crappy TV, and the gray snow gave way to a fuzzy image of my mother, her skin taut as a drumhead as she looked on while some white-coated chef dropped something into a frying pan. Mom and Dad were both wearing aprons, and my mother looked focused but poised, while my father cracked terrible jokes because he was the fun one. It was a rerun, and my parents played the fun-loving, beautifully happy couple to a T. They kept up the act even on current episodes, cooing to each other and launching vaguely sexual (and totally disgusting) zingers.

I snorted when my father made some melon/boob-related comment and my mother pretended to blush. I knew after that episode—after every episode—they would part, come home, and call out to me before retiring to separate studies and eventually separate bedrooms at either end of the house. On air, their loving perfection was palpable, their perfection total.

I'd learned a lot from them.

This stupid cabin barely got cable, let alone cell service, so I was at Rustin's mercy, and now my stomach was growling for something like a cheeseburger. That's what brought me out to the porch. That's why I was opening the door when he was about to knock.

The guy was my dad's age, maybe, with a non-ironic beard and one of those quilted plaid shirts. "Hey…hi."

He smiled and his teeth were faintly yellow, the front one stained with something like nicotine. He was a little twitchy, and each time he moved, I could smell cigarette smoke. I wrinkled my nose.

"Yes? Can I help you with something?"

"You're Hope. Hello." He seemed weirdly pleased, and though I was used to deferential treatment, the guy gave me the heebs, and I closed the door a half inch.

"I think you've got the wrong girl."

I was kicking myself for thinking my lack of makeup was an adequate disguise, but then again, news of my kidnapping had barely been reported, so what did it matter if some creepy lumberjack *maybe* ran into Hope Jensen in the woods? Still, I didn't want to risk it.

"Sorry, buddy."

I went to close the door, but the man reacted swiftly, lodging his boot in the jamb. The door bounced back against his force.

"Yes, you are. I'd know you anywhere. Don't you recognize me?"

His smile was wide and almost desperate. There were white balls of spit on each side of his mouth, and I wanted to gag, to run, to slam the door shut and hide away. Instead, I steeled my resolve, cocked an eyebrow, and popped out my hip.

"I told you… You've got the wrong girl." I kicked at his stupid boot. "Now move your foot."

That big, desperate smile fell from his lips for a millisecond before he dragged a cloudy tongue over his bottom lip. "Aw, come on, Hope. Don't be like that, sweetheart."

It was then that I saw the knife in his hand.

SIXTEEN

Tony

I didn't know if I'd slept. I didn't feel like it; my entire body ached. My head felt like it weighed a thousand pounds, boring into my pillow.

"Are you going to get up?"

Alice was standing in my doorway, dressed for school but barefoot, one small kid foot standing on top of the other. I rolled over to my side, forced a smile I hoped didn't look uncomfortable, and pushed myself to standing.

"Yeah, of course."

"There's cereal for you."

I scooped my little sister up and balanced her on my hip. "You poured cereal?"

She shook her head. "Mommy."

"She's home?"

We turned the corner into the kitchen, and my mom looked over her shoulder. "I'm home. Dad too."

I put Alice down, and she scrambled to her seat, carefully

pushing an overfull bowl of Cheerios toward me. I sat. "Thanks, but I should probably get ready for—"

My mom gestured at me with her coffee mug. "Sit. Eat."

"But—"

"You're not going to school today."

Alice shoved a mammoth spoonful of cereal into her mouth. "Me neither," she said, milk dribbling down her chin.

Mom immediately wiped her up. "Don't talk with your mouth full."

"Why are we not going to school?"

"You're not going to school. Dad and I aren't going to work. We're staying in. Taking a personal family day." Mom smiled, but there was no joy in it.

I turned around in my chair. "Where's Dad?"

"He just went to run an errand. He should be back any time now." A second forced smile, then my mom immediately tried to pour more cereal in my bowl. I covered it with my hands.

"Mom, no. You've poured me like, half a box." I pushed the bowl away. "I'm not even hungry. And I really can't miss school right now." I tried to stand, but my mom put her hands on my shoulders, gently pushing me back down.

"Not today, Tony."

I didn't want to go to school, but I didn't want to stay home either. I wanted everything to be normal, for it to be three days ago, for Hope to not be missing.

No such luck.

I heard the whirl of the cameras, the clicking, before I heard the voices. It sounded like hundreds of them, yelling, getting louder when the door cracked open and my father shimmied through. A man came in behind him.

"Mr. Bellingham."

"Tony." Bellingham crossed the living room and clapped a hand on my shoulder, immediately reaching out to shake my mother's hand. "Lydia." He turned his piercing eyes to Alice. "And you must be little Alice."

Alice shrank back in her chair, plopped another giant spoonful of Cheerios in her mouth, and stared Bellingham down.

"She's harmless, really," I said by way of explanation.

"Alice, why don't you go finish that up in the living room, honey? You can watch cartoons," my mother said.

"I want to watch cartoons with Tony."

My father poured a cup of coffee for Mr. Bellingham and pulled out a chair at the kitchen table for him.

"Honey, Mr. Bellingham is here to talk to Mommy and Daddy and Tony. Can you give us a few minutes?"

Alice pushed out her bottom lip, freckled with Cheerios bits. "Everyone comes to see Tony."

Mr. Bellingham's head snapped toward me. "Who else has come to see you, son?"

Alice slid off her chair, leaving a slosh of Cheerios and milk at her spot. "Hope came to see him last night," she announced as she left the room.

My mother, father, and Bellingham all stared at me, three intent sets of eyes—confused, intrigued, interested.

"Hope was here?" Dad asked.

"Where is she now?" Mom pulled out a chair and sat close enough to brush my shoulder. "Oh, thank God. It's over then, right? Hope's home, she's safe." Then, to me: "She's safe, right? She's home now?"

A lump formed in my throat as I eyed my mom. There were frown lines around her mouth I hadn't noticed before. A deep ridge down the center of her forehead. She just looked *tired*.

I pressed my lips together and shook my head. "No, Ma."

Bellingham pulled his cell phone from his jacket pocket and slid it across the table. "If it were Hope, we would know it."

I glanced down at the picture on Bellingham's screen. It was Everly, from the side, standing at my kitchen window. I was there too, in profile, shadowed. The headline blared: JENSEN STILL MISSING, BOYFRIEND RECEIVES NIGHT VISITOR.

My father paled. My mother's mouth hung open just the smallest bit.

"Tony, what is this about?" my mother asked.

"When... Who is she? Did she come here?" my father added.

Bellingham didn't look the least bit affected. He was not sweating, not a hair was out of place. "I don't know what's happening in the picture, but I can tell you right now that it doesn't really matter. You've heard the expression, 'A picture is worth a thousand words?'"

"Nothing. No, nothing... She just... Her name is Everly, and she was a friend of Hope's. I don't even know why she came over last night." I raked a hand through my hair and felt like it was all about to fall out. "She just wanted to talk."

"She couldn't call?" my father snapped.

"I don't know, Dad—"

"She comes here in the middle of the night?" My mother's voice was strained; she kept picking up her coffee cup and setting it down again without taking a sip. "Don't you know how this looks?"

"It wasn't supposed to look like anything! I didn't invite her to come over! She just showed up!"

"Tony, you need to start being honest with us."

I felt the frustration rising, squeezing the air out of my voice. My chest felt tight. My skin felt hot. "Mr. Bellingham, you have to believe me. She just showed up. She wanted to talk about Hope. She thinks Hope is staging this whole thing." I took a deep breath and glanced from Bellingham to my parents, looking for some shred of evidence that they believed me, that they knew I was telling the truth. "You know me. I'm not… I wouldn't. You know who I am."

There was an impossibly long beat where no one talked but everyone eyed me—Mom, Dad, Bellingham. Blank stares, but something deep in all of them. I felt like I was backpedaling. I felt like I needed to explain myself, but there was nothing to say.

"Guys?"

Finally, my mother reached out. Squeezed my hand. Tears rolled over her cheeks, and her lips were pressed together hard. It ripped at my heart.

Bellingham cleared his throat. "Let me first say this: Everything is going to be okay. I'm going to get you through this. I brought the headline and the picture to your attention because, Tony, you've got to start being really careful right now."

"But I have nothing to do with anything. I'm not even a suspect."

"Not officially, no."

"Well, that should be good enough."

I opened my mouth again, but Bellingham held up a hand. "Regardless, you need to be careful. Don't give them any fodder for their rags. You need to be clean, Tony, pristine clean. I don't care if you have another girlfriend or night visitors, but the public does, and the media is going to run with every little mistake or misstep you make."

I wanted to defend myself, but I thought better of it.

"So no more talking to anyone other than me and this family unless you run it by me first, clear?"

I nodded, numb.

"We're going to cooperate with the police. We're going to issue a statement."

My stomach dropped into my shoes. "A statement of what? I haven't done anything."

"Mr. Bellingham…" my mother started, her voice strangely high. "Is Tony actually going to be arrested?"

It took forever for Bellingham to nod his head. "If he's not now, he's going to be any minute. We're going to go down to the police station in a show of good faith. Tony will be able to tell his side of the story."

"I don't even have a side. And I told them, like, three times already. I was talking to Hope on the phone. I heard her scream… the tires squealing… That was all. That's everything."

Hope's voice reverberated back to me, sounding hollow and

tinny in my own mind. The screech of the tires cut through the gnat-buzzing hum in my head.

"It wasn't me."

"And that's what we're going to be sure to tell the police. You're going to be helpful, Tony. It's going to be scary. They're going to want to search your car, your room, likely even your house, Mr. and Mrs. Gardner. Now, Tony…" Bellingham's eyes went an intense, piercing blue. "Is there anything you need to tell me before this happens?"

I thought about the websites. I thought about Hope.

"Our love is a flower that blooms…"

The peals of hyena-like laughter.

The screech of the tires.

"If there is anything that you would like me to hold for safekeeping…"

Share Location? The throbbing cursor.

"Mr. Bellingham, sir, I don't think I like what you're implying. Our son has nothing to hide. If he says he didn't have anything to do with Hope's disappearance"—my mother gasped slightly, lost her words, then seemed to regain her composure—"he didn't."

I thought of my laptop sitting on my desk. I thought of my search history, of Hope's phone. I thought of the message from RIDETHEWAVE.

Gotcha.

My stomach was in knots. I stood.

"Tony, honey, you don't look so good."

I sprinted to the bathroom and slammed the door, sinking onto the cool linoleum. My gut continued to churn, the sick feeling creeping up the back of my neck. I was sweating so much I could feel it dripping down my back and front, dampening the waistband of my sweatpants. I crawled to the toilet and tried to throw up, but nothing came out. The water just swirled in front of my eyes.

Come clean.

I have to just come clean, to tell them everything.

Then everything will be okay.

Mr. Bellingham…

Share Location?

She deserved it.

I gripped the sides of the toilet, and my stomach recoiled.

She deserved it.

Afterward, I filled a glass of water and swished the taste of vomit out of my mouth. My mother knocked on the door. "Tony, honey, are you okay?"

Sat back onto the floor. Rolled onto my side. Let the cool of the linoleum soak through my sweatshirt. I stared at the water in my water glass.

I wasn't okay.

SEVENTEEN

I stood on Renee Wright's porch, counting the bongs from her fancy doorbell. Inside, a dog barked, and five minutes seemed to pass before I heard the lock tumble and Renee pulled open the door. Her face tightened when she saw it was me.

"What are you doing here?"

"I know you talked to Hope that night."

Renee glanced over her shoulder, then slipped out the door and joined me on the porch, her arms crossed in front of her chest. "No I didn't."

"I know you did, Renee. I just need to know what Hope said."

"I don't know what you're talking about, Tony. The last time I talked to Hope was at school that day."

I tried to stare her down. "I know you talked to her. Five times. She called you three times, and you called her twice, right around nine and ten o'clock."

"I worked until ten o'clock that night. And if you weren't with Hope, how are you so sure I even talked to her?"

"I saw her phone! I saw your number come up on her phone."

I could see the cogs moving in Renee's head. "When did you see her phone?"

I bit my lip. "I went to her house after I talked to her, okay? She wasn't there, but her phone was. I looked at the call log."

I stared Renee down, watching for her facade to crack, for some tiny twinge that would tell me she was lying and let me in on Hope's big joke. Instead, her eyes widened and her cheeks flushed hot pink.

"You found her phone? She left her phone?" Renee's eyes went glassy, and tears started spilling over her cheeks. "Oh my God, oh my God, did you tell the police?"

I could feel the panic rising in my chest. Renee was either really terrified or a really great actress. "I saw that you called her. RR… It was on her phone."

"I'm not RR, I'm RW. Renee Wright. Wright, with a *W*." Renee sniffed. "Who's RR?"

EIGHTEEN

I watched Rustin Rice shoulder his backpack, wave good-bye to a few friends, then make his way toward the student lot. I jogged over to him, and he glanced at me, clearly startled.

"What do you want?" he mumbled.

I shrugged, doing my best nonchalant act. "Nothing."

"All right. Bye." Rustin turned his back to me.

"Just one question, bro."

Rustin turned and eyed me, one strawberry-blond eyebrow cocked. "Yeah?"

"You talk to Hope lately?" I kept my eyes on him, scrutinizing, looking for some sign that he was about to crack or admit the truth.

A noncommittal shrug. "Not really. You know she's missing, right?"

"It's all over the news."

"So how would I have talked to her?" His face was stone—no flinch, no shifty eyes. Not that I really knew what to look for.

"I don't know. I thought you guys were getting pretty close…"

"You guys weren't seeing each other anymore."

"I know. But after."

Rustin shifted his weight, his chest hefting out a tiny bit more. "What are you getting at, dude?"

I had to admit I had no idea what I was doing, what I was expecting. That Rustin would fall to his knees, suddenly crumble, and admit that Hope was stashed in his closet or something?

"Never mind, man."

I walked to my car feeling stupid and defeated, but I didn't start the engine. Instead, I watched Rustin walk to his, then pulled into the lane of traffic three cars behind him. I followed him for six miles, hiding behind a minivan plastered with an enormous stick-figure family and an Entenmann's snack cake truck. Rustin pulled off the highway and I followed, taking two corners and eventually flicking on my blinker a car length behind him.

I followed Rustin into the 7-Eleven parking lot, then into the store. He didn't notice me because he was on his phone the whole time, a basket slung over one arm, raking things off the shelf. When he finally slid the phone into his back pocket, I was about to make my move. But then I noticed the things he was putting in his basket: Baby carrots. Hummus. Coconut water.

Rustin was kind of an athlete—the kind who was naturally good at sports and ate two of everything at one sitting at McDonald's. Not the hummus and coconut-water type. Not baby carrots. I followed behind him and paused when he paused at the stand of sad-looking leftover fruit. I watched him inspect the bananas and poke at a soft spot on an apple that had seen better days. Finally, he went for the package of blueberry muffins hanging from the side of the produce cart.

I shook my head. "She's not going to eat those, dude."

He looked up, surprised to see me. "What?" Then back to the muffins. "What are you muttering about, Gardner?"

"Hope. Hates anything full-sized that's prepackaged and artificial. And those"—I pointed—"have been here since freshman year. Best bet is try the mini muffins. She usually lets those slide based on the cute factor."

Rustin looked at me, half incredulous, half annoyed. "What the hell do you know about it?"

I shrugged. "Just saying."

"And who says I'm getting these for Hope? I told you, we weren't doing anything. I don't know where she is. No one does, man." He squashed the muffins back onto the shelf and took a step closer to me, so we were nearly chest to chest. "Unless you have something to confess."

I was trying to keep my cool, but I could feel the perspiration beading under my arms, and my palms were slick and wet. I held them up anyway, hoped the expression on my face was even and unfazed. "I'm just trying to help."

Rustin held my stare for a beat before halfheartedly lunging at me, then jumping back. I held my ground, even through my heart was whaling in my throat. He offered one of those stupid dude chuckles.

"Fuck off, Gardner."

I left the 7-Eleven and sat in my car, waiting. Inside, Rustin looked around before slipping a package of mini muffins into his basket and moving through the checkout line.

I slid low in the driver's seat, threw on a baseball hat, and pulled out my cell phone.

Bellingham answered on the first ring.

"Hey, it's Tony. I've got some information for you."

Bellingham sounded wary. "What kind of information?"

"About Hope. I think…I think she's hiding out somewhere. You know, holed up, pulling the strings?"

I could almost hear him lean into the phone. "What do you know?"

"There's this kid from school, Rustin Rice. I know he knows Hope. Anyway, I heard him say some stuff at school, then I followed him here to the 7-Eleven. He was grocery shopping." I paused.

"And?"

"Well, he bought hummus, baby carrots, coconut water, and mini muffins."

"So he likes tiny things. That's not a crime."

"No, he wasn't shopping for himself. The kid is a human garbage disposal. What teenage guy do you know eats baby carrots?"

"Frankly, I don't know and I don't care."

I blew out a frustrated sigh. "You don't get it."

"Obviously. Explain it to me, or quite wasting my time. Your case isn't going to hinge on baby vegetables."

"Hope loves all those things. And when I confronted Rustin— because he got regular-sized muffins and Hope won't eat those—he changed to the mini muffins."

"And?" I could tell that Bellingham wasn't following my mode of thinking, and I was almost swayed.

"Don't you see? He's buying stuff to bring to Hope, wherever she is. He knows, obviously."

"Because he bought some mini muffins?"

"You don't know Hope."

"Did this kid actually say he knew where Hope was? Or that the crap he was buying was for her?"

"No, but—"

"Tony, look, I appreciate what you're trying to do, but the best thing you can do for yourself, your case—hell, for Hope—is to lie low. Just go home and keep out of sight."

I was trying to listen to Bellingham, but Rustin stepped out of the store with his paper bag and tossed it on the passenger seat of his car.

"He's leaving now," I said.

"Who?"

"Rustin. I'm going to follow him."

"No, you're not. You're going to go home."

"He's probably going right to her."

"Tony, go home."

But I'd already fed the key into the ignition and turned the engine over. Rustin was backing out, and I waited a beat, then followed a car length behind him. He seemed to already have forgotten me, cranking up his radio so Pitbull came screaming out the windows.

"I'll call you later, Bellingham."

I followed Rustin for three miles down the expressway, losing hope. He was heading toward his house. Maybe he was just a baby carrot–eating douche, and I was the idiot wasting my time following him around town.

But then he threw his blinker on.

Made a left turn.

Got on the freeway.

He hit seventy, seventy-five in the blink of an eye. His BMW purred like a kitten; my geriatric Corolla spat and shimmied, rpms rising with an unhealthy-sounding groan. I was waiting for my engine to blow, for smoke to start spewing, when Rustin took a hard right turn, catching an exit. I slammed on my brakes and did the same, my car whinnying, my tires spitting out gravel like gunfire. He took the off ramp smoothly; I took it with an inelegant *eeek* and a cloud of dust, but I could still see his bright taillights and the slick black bumper of his fancy car.

And then I saw the brake lights.

My stomach dropped, and pins and needles shot out across my body. I slammed my foot on the brake, and my eyes closed at the same time as I cursed myself and tried to wrench my eyes back open.

I smelled the burned rubber. The smoke and grit from the road floated into my open car windows and choked me. I slid for what felt like a football field, coughing, choking, leg fully extended, knee locked, brake pedal mashed against the car mat, hands gripping the wheel. Rustin was outside his car, watching mine slide, his face barely registering a centimeter of tension as the bumper of my car came to within inches of his brand-new one.

He let out a breath when I came to a cloudy stop, my whole

dashboard shimmying, my steering wheel bucking, my heart slamming against my rib cage. I pushed my car into park at the same time that Rustin wrenched my car door open, clapped a hand onto my chest, and yanked me out by my T-shirt.

"What the fuck was that, you idiot? You following me?" He shoved me against my own car, and I sprawled like a boneless stuffed toy. It wasn't that Rustin was all that strong; it was that there was nothing in my body—no bones, nothing but white-hot lactic acid that pooled in my muscles and made me an uncoordinated idiot. That was why I didn't move when he punched me. Square in the jaw. My mouth exploded with blood, a starburst of pain, and before I knew it, I was hitting back. I had Rustin by the shirtfront, my knuckles crashing against his cheek. His head vaulted back, and I got a spray of blood-tinged saliva.

"Where's Hope, you asshole? Where is she?"

I hit again, and Rustin went from solid to deadweight. I was holding him up by his T-shirt as his knees buckled underneath him. I coiled back for another punch, but he had his hands up. He wasn't giving up; he was going in for another shot. It caught me in the chest, and I heard myself let out a groan, my hands going to my belly. Rustin stumbled back, recoiled, and came at me hard.

That was why I didn't hear the sirens.

We were lodged together, fighting, punching, scrabbling.

That was why I didn't hear the officers' voices.

My fist hit the fleshy part of Rustin's gut.

That was why I didn't feel the arms on me, the hands, until I felt the cold clink of metal around my wrist. Until I felt my shoulder screaming, my other arm being wrenched behind my back.

The cops pulled me and Rustin apart, and we were both breathing hard, slightly hunched, arms pinned behind our backs. Rustin had blood on his shirt. A busted lip. His teeth and gums were bloody. I didn't remember hitting him that hard, that much, but he looked bad.

"Gardner." It was Pace. If I'd had anything left to lose, it would have shown, but I didn't. Instead, I sighed, little bits of snot and blood raining out of my nose. I could taste the blood on my lips.

"It's not what it looks like."

Pace didn't bother to answer, just cocked an eyebrow and looked from me to Rustin. "This psychopath has been following me all day," he spat out.

MacNamara was there too, walking up slowly, notebook out and poised. I could hear her walkie-talkie cackling on her shoulder, and I watched as she leaned into it, murmured something. I couldn't make much of it out, but two words stood out loud and clear: Tony Gardner.

"I only followed him from the 7-Eleven," I said, keeping my voice low. Every breath I took made my lungs wheeze and felt like my rib cage was shrinking in on itself.

"Why were you following him at all?" MacNamara wanted to know.

"Because he's picking things up for Hope. He knows where she is. Admit it, Rustin. You know where Hope is, and you're bringing her supplies."

MacNamara and Pace swung to look at Rustin. "This true?"

Rustin paused long enough to spit out a mouthful of blood and saliva. "No."

I tried to step forward, but Pace pushed me back. "He has groceries in his car. Check inside! He's got a bag of supplies!"

MacNamara took her time walking toward Rustin's car, scanning the inside. "I see a grocery bag."

"I bought some groceries."

"For Hope!" I shouted.

"For my mom!" Rustin shouted back.

I felt like I was been pummeled again. "No…the muffins. He has mini muffins!"

MacNamara raised her eyebrows, hand on the driver's side door.

"Go ahead," Rustin told her. She slid the grocery bag over.

"He does have mini muffins."

"Yeah, my mom likes mini muffins." Rustin looked from one officer to another. "That's a crime?"

"He bought them for Hope!"

"Did you buy some mini muffins for your friend Hope, son?"

"No."

Pace shrugged, didn't try to hide his smile. "Seems airtight to me."

I looked incredulously from Pace to MacNamara. "You can't just—" But then I heard how ridiculous it sounded. How futile. How stupid.

I'd beaten up a guy and was standing on the side of the road in handcuffs over a goddamn package of blueberry mini muffins.

I was going to jail.

NINETEEN
THREE DAYS MISSING

Hope

I'm not afraid of anything, which is why when the man lunged for me, I didn't take off running. I didn't kick him or clomp on the soft spot on the top of his foot like I'd been trained in a series of half-assed self-defense classes the school made the girls take for a P.E. unit.

Yeah, I saw the knife. It was an ordinary kitchen knife, and maybe it didn't scare me much because my brain just wondered what the hell he was thinking of chopping way out here in the woods.

And then he was in the house.

He was inches from me, and I could smell him—sweat, dirt, something weird and metallic I couldn't recognize. There was a sheen of sweat across his face that made the dirty spots on his cheeks glisten, and the hiss of his breath was hot and foul.

"Hey…"

He reached for me, his thin and papery fingertips catching me at my collarbone, then arching into claws and raking over the bare skin, his fingernails digging in, leaving a trail of hot fire. I stumbled backward, instinctively pushing out as he reached in. My palms slammed against his chest, and it was hard, solid, not what I expected. He was immovable, everything except the expression on his face. His lips curved up like a sick gargoyle, and there was light in his mud-brown eyes—and suddenly I realized he was *enjoying* this.

"Hope!"

He was fast too, faster than he should have been for an old, dirty, wrinkled man, and when I turned, I heard his hand slice the air a hairbreadth from my ear. The *swoosh* of it lifted the baby hairs that stuck to the sweat along the back of my neck. His other hand landed hard on my shoulder, slamming down so hard that I winced, a sharp, little *Oy* that came from somewhere way low in my belly. He was ripping at me, clawing at my jeans, at the hood of my sweatshirt. He caught me, and the zipper tightened around my neck, burning at my throat.

I clawed at my own chest, feeling my nails digging into flesh as I ripped at the zipper, wriggled out of my sweatshirt, and left him holding it as my feet registered on the hardwood floor. I slipped at first, and my legs went from heavy and leaden to thin and lighter than I'd ever felt them—and I was running for my life. My thighs burned and my fingernails dug blood from my palms as I clenched my fists and pumped myself forward, forward.

"Leave me alone! Get the hell away from me!"

It occurred to me that I didn't know this house, that I didn't know where to go. I was drawing a blank as I was running just back, just away, and he was gaining on me, kicking aside the coffee table and smashing into a chair that splintered against the edge of the fireplace. I didn't think I stopped, but I must have, because he closed the distance and then I was flying, light again, sailing, until I heard the ugly crush of bone against hardwood.

My chin hit the floor. My teeth rattled and clenched against a flood of hot velvet blood. My head, my head… It was in slow motion. The last few inches of the tiny wood-flanked living room pitching sideways, the starburst explosion of pain behind my right eye, the cool rush of blood down my cheek, and then everything went dark.

TWENTY

Tony

Bellingham was disgusted and didn't even try to hide it. My mother was wringing her hands in her lap. My father shifted a sleeping Alice from one hip to the other. We were at the police station. Lights were flashing, and people were peering in through the windows. I didn't know where they were holding Rustin, or if they had let him go. On the side of the highway, Pace had bowed my head, locked me into the squad car, and pulled into traffic while MacNamara talked to Rustin. He was still in cuffs, and she was taking notes in her little black book.

That couldn't have been more than an hour ago, but it looked like every reporter in three states had heard the news and converged on the police station. At first, I thought some celebrity must have gotten arrested or some serial killer was on the loose. When we drove up and the flashes turned on Pace's car, he chuckled and let me know that now I was a star.

We sat in a police waiting room in awkward silence.

"What were you even thinking, Tony?" My mother's voice was soft when she finally did speak. I wished I had other explanation rather than "I saw some mini muffins and went crazy."

"We're not going to be able to keep this off the news, are we?" My dad's voice was low.

"It was on the news before the cuffs ever hit Tony's wrists." Bellingham raked a hand through his hair, and I was struck by how old he looked now. Like my parents: aged twenty years overnight. Because of me.

Because of Hope.

I could feel the lump at the back of my throat, tears pricking my eyes. I looked at the stupid, slick gray ceiling of the police station and wished I were dead, blinking hard so I didn't cry.

Bellingham stood. "Wait right here."

We waited for what seemed like an eternity. I counted the ceiling tiles and listened to the whoosh and whirl of Alice's breath as she slept. Finally, Bellingham came out.

"We can go."

I blinked, shocked. "What?"

"Pace said we can go."

My mother stood. "So this boy isn't pressing charges?"

"Not exactly. They're not pressing charges at this time and releasing Tony into our custody."

I almost smiled, but Bellingham ran on.

"...as long as we come back within twenty-four hours to give a formal statement to the police."

"I've talked to the police already," I said.

My dad's look was fierce. "You'll do what Mr. Bellingham suggests, Tony." He turned abruptly, my mother taking one quick look back before following him toward the door.

Finally, she reached out for me. "Come on, Tony."

I took one last, sweeping look at the 127 ceiling tiles in the police department waiting room.

Two weeks ago, I didn't even know there were ceiling tiles in this place.

I barely even knew this place existed.

Now I was a regular with a lawyer and a couple of parents who could barely look at me—and when they did, they shook their heads in disbelief or said things like "Tony, what is going on with you?"

What the hell *was* going on with me?

I don't wonder for long. She was always behind it. Always.

Hope.

TWENTY-ONE
THREE DAYS MISSING

Hope

I wasn't in Rustin's parents' cabin anymore. I was in a fun house. The edges of everything—the furniture, the walls, the ugly stone fireplace—all seemed rounded and cartoonish and soft. I wanted to touch everything to see if they actually were soft, but either my brain couldn't find my fingers or my fingers couldn't find my brain because nothing happened.

And then I saw the boots—muddy, huge, slow and plodding—moving toward me. With every step, my brain vibrated. My teeth rattled. A new rivulet of blood filled my mouth. I was lying on my side, and every step he took shook the cheap plank-wood floor. I wanted to close my eyes and drift into that feelingless blackness again, but it was as if my eyes had been peeled open. As with my fingers, I couldn't move my eyes. I couldn't shut them. I couldn't shut off the boots that were one foot away. Six inches. So close that I could nudge the rounded steel-toed end with my nose.

The man crouched, and I willed my body to arch, to move, to

jump back so he couldn't touch me but nothing, not a damn thing, happened.

The man must have been reading my mind because he smiled. Another of those grotesque, gargoyle-like smiles that curved the edges of his thin, greasy lips.

"You're awake."

I opened my mouth to speak, but my words were garbled, strangled.

He cocked his head. "Aw, let me help you with that."

I could feel the sweat bead as his fingers moved close to my face. His fingernails were even and well manicured, but my stomach still lurched when they touched my face. The man moved my hair from my cheek and then pinched my skin with those nails, and my jaw hung open.

He pushed the saliva-soaked gag down my chin, and suddenly I was gasping, sucking in air, but every bone in my face ached. I felt like I've been punched and wondered vaguely if I had been. I breathed for a second before the anger overwhelmed me.

"Who the fuck are you? What the fuck do you want with me? Let me go, you crazy fuck!" My voice was tinny, ragged.

The man cocked his head again, looking completely unfazed. He clicked his tongue. "That language is not becoming a lady, Hope."

Bile itched at the back of my throat.

I didn't want him to say my name. He shouldn't be allowed to say my name.

Those thin, greasy lips. His yellowed teeth.

He can't say my name.

A sob lodged in my throat, but I refused to cry. I wouldn't let him see me cry. "How do you know my name? How do you know who I am?"

"I know everything about you, Hope."

His voice was unnervingly serene.

"How?"

He sighed and sank back on the arm of the couch, staring down at me. Still, he smiled. I wanted to throw up, spit, claw his eyes out.

"You invited me."

The fog in my head was starting to thin—slowly, agonizingly slowly. I was trying to focus on him, to commit his horrible face to memory or to jar something loose… Did I know him? Did I recognize this guy? I was sure that I didn't.

"I didn't invite you. I don't fucking know who you are."

"Language, Hope."

"How did you even find me?" I thought of Rustin's cabin, of the drive deeper and deeper into the woods.

"I always know where you are. I watch you. I've been watching you." He puffed out his chest. "It's my job." Then, a half whisper as he leaned into me: "I'm real good at it."

"Who *are* you?" I spat out.

He looked genuinely pleased, like we were having a normal conversation over a couple of lattes, and I wasn't hog-tied on a filthy wooden floor in some old house.

"Now that's how to talk to a friend. Call me Daniel."

Daniel. *Daniel.* Daniel. I turned the name over and over in my head, held it on my tongue, forced my brain to recognize it. *Do I know a Daniel? Do my parents know Daniel?*

"Do you work on the show?"

Daniel crossed his arms in front of his chest, pushed out those boots again, and crossed his legs at the ankles. His socks were stark white, carefully folded down. "Not exactly. Your parents are phonies."

For some reason, a lump swelled in my throat, and I could feel tears prick at the edges of my eyes.

"Don't worry," Daniel told me. "You won't have to deal with them anymore."

I blinked, desperate to stop the flood of tears that threatened to fall. "What are you talking about?"

He shrugged, ignoring my question. "This is nice. I knew you were nice."

Thoughts raced through my head, slamming me behind the eyes. *Spit. Scream. Damn him to hell. Get the fuck out of here. Kill him.*

Focus, Hope.

"It would be nice if you would untie me."

Daniel dragged his tongue across his lips, and I couldn't help but watch the snail trail of saliva while my stomach threatened to wretch.

"I don't know, Hope. Can I trust you?"

You have me fucking hog-tied on the floor of some godforsaken house, and you want me to trust you, you freakazoid? I was desperate to shout, to snap at him, to snap him in half.

Instead, I forced myself to nod, the action miniscule as every move, no matter how minor, pulled and tightened the ropes' course across my body.

"You can trust me. I'm not going to do anything." I widened my eyes, hoped they look pleading and sweet.

Daniel started to soften, and he came at me again with those coarse hands. I couldn't help but flinch. He noticed.

The light flush in his cheeks went to full, rageful red. His nostrils flared. His lips curled and his teeth were exposed, bared like a snarling wolfhound's, and I heard the smack of skin on skin before I felt the burn that tore across my nose, shredding my lip.

"I disgust you, is that it?" His voice was a low growl.

"No, no," I shook my head, then flinched again, the tears rushing over my cheeks as the blood pooled behind my teeth. "Please untie me. Please, Daniel, just a little bit. This hurts. It really hurts! I'm not disgusted by you… You just…you…" I sniffled. "You just scared me is all. You have me tied up here and on the floor…"

Immediately Daniel dropped to his knees and started to fidget with the ropes. I wasn't sure if he was trying to strangle me or help me. Panic flared through me, my skin tightening, my eyes bulging. I wanted to scream, to struggle, to fight back, but the will was paralyzed inside me.

Move, damn it!

React, Hope!

With each move Daniel made, another millimeter of the rope dug into my throat, cut at the skin on my wrists and ankles. I felt blood bubbling, felt the itching trails as red slid from my damaged flesh.

"Please, Daniel, please."

"I'm not going to hurt you, Hope. I would never hurt you. You're my special girl. You're a special little girl."

I saw the knife in Daniel's hand. It was the same blade from before, dull, aged, and my heart slammed against my rib cage.

He was going to kill me.

"Oh God, please no, please, no!"

Daniel stopped, staring from the knife to me. I could see his eyes—dull, blank, and shallow—reflected in the blade.

I'm not afraid of anything.

Or anyone.

But Daniel...

He had that knife in his hand. Twisting it, flipping it. I couldn't keep my eyes off the blade, but he wasn't even looking at it, just staring at me the whole time, dragging that tongue across his lips. I could hear him breathe. Every inch he moved closer to me was an invasion of my personal space. I wanted to say something, but all I could do was focus on that blade. *Slip, roll, slide.*

Slip, roll, slide.

"I've waited so long for us to be together like this, Hope."

He paused, waited for me to answer, but everything inside me was trembling, no matter how hard I clenched everything down, shut everything down. I could feel the blood burning through my veins and pooling in my muscles.

"I don't even know who you are."

I could see from the corner of my eye as Daniel's chin dropped.

"Well, that makes me a little sad. But you weren't ever that observant. You always had so much going on."

Slip, roll, slide.

"You had your friends and that boyfriend around all the time…"

Tony. I felt myself flinch.

Daniel did something between a snort and a chuckle. "All the boys were always around you. Then again…" He stopped, shuffling the knife and pinned me with a gross, dead-eyed stare. "I can't blame them. You're an angel." He took a single index finger and dragged it down my bare skin. It felt like fire. It felt like I was going to split open at the seams. My stomach roiled.

"Just so beautiful."

I shrank back, putting as much distance between Daniel and me as I could. "What are you going to do with me?"

Daniel actually seemed taken aback. *Pleased*, even. I wanted to throw up. I wanted to gnash my teeth, sink them into him, and tear his flesh apart—but I didn't even want to touch him.

"Well, Hope. I was hoping we'd get to this point. You, interested in me."

I was aghast. How the hell could he think I was interested in *him*? I eyed the knife again, and Daniel laughed. "Oh! You want to know what I'm going to do with this?" He brandished the thing, waved it a quarter inch from my nose. I could actually smell the cold metal. "That's what you're interested in! Well, Hope, I guess, when it comes to us"—he pointed the knife first at his chest, then mine—"you and me and this"—again with the knife—"well, I guess a lot of that is up to you."

I sucked in a long, low breath. "Well, if a lot of that is up to me, I want you to let me go."

Daniel blinked at me. "But we've just barely begun."

I steeled myself, confidence coming out of nowhere. "Let. Me. Go."

His expression darkened. "Not after how hard I've worked to get you here. You're going to love it, Hope, I promise. You're going to love it, and love me, and we're going—"

The spit stopped him midsentence.

His nostrils flared, and fire raged in his eyes. "How dare you!"

I saw the knife in his hand. I saw him rear back. I flinched, mashing myself against the wall, holding my breath. I waited for the blade. For my flesh to slash open. I didn't expect the wallop.

The heel of Daniel's hand came down hard across my right cheek. I was sure every tooth was broken. I could feel the blood gush from my nose, the tears welling in my eyes and pouring down my cheeks.

Daniel sat back with a slight, satisfied grin.

I pounced.

Used every ounce of energy I had and lurched toward him, blood-covered hands clawed. I would get out of this house if it killed me. I would get back to my parents, to Tony, to my school. I would survive.

TWENTY-TWO

Tony

I couldn't figure Bellingham out.

"Why do you want to help me?" I asked him as we crossed the parking lot to his car. "You know I can't even pay you."

"It's not about the money," he said, walking with a motivated stride. "And pay them no mind." He jutted his chin toward two reporters loitering at the edge of the parking lot. I stared at the concrete while they snapped pictures, then dared a glance up. Bellingham was mugging for them. Not smiling, but a stern lawyer-with-a-purpose look. "We have no comments," he announced, though no one asked. Suddenly I felt a little less like Bellingham's charity case and more like his meal ticket.

Like Hope.

I bit down the thought.

Bellingham stopped in front of a gray sedan that looked like every other gray sedan ever. He clicked the alarm and grinned. "I'm between luxury vehicles right now." I sat down; the car was neat, newly vacuumed, equipped with a little garbage bag filled with water bottles. But as clean as the car was, the interior still bore the same faint fried-chicken smell of his office.

I hoped the smell wasn't catching.

After I showered that morning, I went into my room and saw that my mother had laid out something for me to wear: the navy-blue slacks that had sat in my closet for a year after my cousin's wedding and a white button-down shirt. When I was dressed and in the living room, she told me Bellingham had picked out the outfit. He said we were presenting an image. *We* like we were in this together, like we would both be interrogated and sent to jail, *we* like both of our lives were on trial for a girl who may or may not even be missing.

"Look, is there anything else you need to tell me before we arrive?"

My parents were driving behind us; I watched them turn off one exit earlier to drop Alice off at my aunt's.

"Do you want to know if I'm guilty?" I asked.

Again, Bellingham held out one of his famous I-don't-want-to-hear-it hands. "That's not relevant. Is there anything the police might know that I don't? Another girl in the bushes perhaps?"

Anger roiled at the base of my spine. "I didn't invite her. Or expect her. She just kind of showed up. I had barely even spoken to Everly before any of this. She came by because…"

Bellingham switched gears so that the car jerked a tiny bit and the rpms revved. I gripped the seat and swallowed hard.

"Because why?"

"She thinks that Hope isn't missing."

He looked at me and cocked an eyebrow. I wished he'd keep his eyes on the road. "I know you think that, but—"

"Everly thinks that Hope planned this whole thing. That she didn't really get kidnapped."

"She'd do that, what, for publicity?"

I paused for a beat. "For revenge."

"'Cuz of your whole breakup thing?" Bellingham actually chuckled. "That'd be pretty rich."

"It's not that far-fetched."

"Hope's a kid."

The anger was welling up further, a snake climbing up each vertebra. "Hope's a kid with a lot of money. Resources." I looked out the window. "Rage issues. You'd be amazed at the things she's capable of. Especially when she's bored."

"So according to this Everly person, Hope is staging the whole thing. Was never really in any danger to begin with. What's she going to do? End the whole thing with a big ta-da? Told you so? Parade or something?"

I shifted in my seat. "I don't know. I don't know why Hope did half the stuff that she did. But don't you think it's possible? Even a little bit?"

Bellingham thought for a beat, then nodded his head slowly. "I've been married three times. I don't put any kind of bizarre behavior past a woman. Particularly past a woman seeking revenge. This could be an angle we could play. You think Everly would be willing to talk to the police?"

"She seemed eager to talk that night. She seemed like she wanted to help me."

Bellingham cocked his head as we exited the freeway. My eyes coasted over the bright-blue Police Department sign with the white arrow. My stomach twisted again, and I reminded myself that it was empty. I didn't have anything left to throw up.

"That's nice. Little lady wants to do something nice for you."

"She's not doing something nice. She knows Hope. She knows that lying is definitely in Hope's wheelhouse. Don't you see where it could be possible?"

Bellingham flicked on his blinker; it was smooth and almost soundless.

"Absolutely. But we're going to have a hard time building a case. Seen the Jensens' morning show? They've all but painted a halo on that kid. Right now she's a missing angel, all white and ethereal and saving puppies."

"Hope hates dogs."

"Didn't she volunteer at the pound?"

"She paid people to volunteer for her."

Bellingham snort-chuckled. "I like you, kid. We need to get the whole town to like you just as much as they like the Jensen kid."

"I'm nobody though. I don't do anything but go to school and work. I don't… My parents don't have a show or anything. I'm just…" I looked down, barely recognizing myself in the crisp, white button-down and the stupid navy-blue pants with sharp-as-knives pleats. "Why are people going to care about me?"

"Because we're going to introduce them to who you really are and to who Hope really is."

I let that sink in for a minute.

"Keep your window up and your head down, kid. Those two reporters before were just the warm-up."

Bellingham unlocked the doors with a sharp click, and the silence enveloped me for a half second before he pulled open my car door. Then there were people crowded in front of me. Cameras, microphones, cell phones. People yelling, snapping. They knew my name. They called me *Tony* and *Mr. Gardner*.

They asked me where Hope was.

Bellingham snapped through the haze and grabbed my arm, pulling me out of the car. I stumbled a few steps and blinked in the overbright sunlight. He held an arm up in front of him and used his other hand to force my head down a bit so I was staring at my shoes, following along behind him like some kind of bewildered lapdog.

Actually, that's exactly how I felt.

I was relieved when we got through the double glass doors of the police station because once they snapped shut, the outside world was cut off. I wondered why they didn't just follow us in, but the reporters stayed back, staring at me through their lenses, and for that I was grateful. I glanced around and noticed there were other people in the crowd too, some with handmade signs. HOPE in glittery letters. A close-up of Hope's face cut from the newspaper. A woman, silent, grimaced at me through the glass. Her hands were clenched hard on either side of a piece of poster board. The only thing written across it was the word *Murderer*.

My throat went bone dry.

"Hey, just don't look at them, okay?" It was Bellingham, his voice gruff in my ear.

I nodded mutely but spun back to the assembled crowd when I heard them start to chatter. It was because of my parents. They were pushing through the crowd, heads down, but even so, I could see my mother's drawn lips, the pale hollow of my father's cheeks. Bellingham made his way to the door, and the shouts of the reporters wafted into the police station vestibule.

"Has your son admitted anything to you?"

"Do you know Hope Jensen?"

"Mr. and Mrs. Gardner, how do you feel knowing that Tony is a suspect?"

Something cold and wet sat at the base of my spine. I went to turn around, but before I did, she caught my eye.

Everly.

Standing next to the silent lady with the Murderer sign. Everly's expression was blank, her blue eyes wide and open. She held up a fist and opened it. Waved hello without a smile.

"That's Everly. That's the girl from last night," I told Mr. Bellingham.

His gaze went directly to her, laser focused. "She's just blending into the crowd right now. Don't make eye contact. As far as you're concerned, you don't know her, have never seen her, have no idea why she's here."

"I really don't have any idea why she's here. But maybe she could talk to the police... Tell them what she told me."

Bellingham took my arm. "Doesn't work like that. This is about you, us, right now." He nodded at each of my parents. "Mr. and Mrs. Gardner, this is just routine. I'll have Tony in and out of here in just a few minutes. The paperwork might take a little longer, but I'll keep you updated on everything. Please, make yourselves comfortable."

Turning to the assembled crowd at the police station was only minimally better than facing the crowd outside. The cops in front of me were all uniformed and professional looking. No one jutted out with arms raised; no cell phones waved in my face. No one yelled my name or snapped a picture, but the silence was worse.

The woman at the desk in front of me. The guy standing to her left. The two working at hulking metal desks who pretended that they weren't glancing over the tops of their computer screens at me. I felt like I could see the cogs turning in their brains as they sized me up, matched me against all the other suspects they'd seen in this precinct, wondering if I was capable of murder.

"I didn't do anything," I found myself whispering, a pitiful, strained sound. I could feel the blood pulsing in my cheeks, could feel the sweat starting up again. I could smell myself, and I realized with sickening dread that what I was smelling was fear—my own.

"I didn't do anything," I mumbled again.

TWENTY-THREE

Hope

My head was throbbing. My whole body felt like it was made out of papier-mâché, shattered, then slapped back together again with newspaper and globs of starch. Everything hurt. My teeth. My neck, my head… Hell, even my *hair* hurt. I tried to shift, and then everything was worse.

I tried to open my eyes, but they felt like they were glued shut. When I finally got my lashes apart and blinked—then blinked again—a shower of something like fine sawdust dotted my cheeks. Shards fell into my eyes. Bright red. Bloodred. It was then I tasted the blood in my mouth and could smell it everywhere.

My whole body pricked awake. Skin that felt like it was already too tight tightened again. I tried to shift, tried to break the black streak of pain that darted down my spine. I tried to straighten, but something dug into my neck, into the soft skin around my throat.

Rope.

"And that's our little Hope, right there, our little graduate!"

I worked to straighten, despite the shot of pain that bolted through me. "Mom?"

Her voice sounded different, higher, sweeter—her television voice.

"She goes right up to the principal and grabs her diploma… See right there? Our little Hope! She's not afraid. Most of the other little kids are afraid, but not our Hope. She just marches right across that stage!"

There was a television on. That was the faint light glowing from the corner. I fixed my eyes and I could see it, the grainy picture from the home movie: our home movie. *My* home movie. My kindergarten graduation. I was wearing a red polka-dotted dress with a crisp, white apron over the top, edged with red rickrack and strawberries. I was wearing a red construction-paper mortarboard with a green yarn tassel.

My parents weren't in the room. They weren't at the graduation. They were commenting on me, their brave little Hope onstage, from their spots on the morning show stage. I'd seen this episode. I took my diploma, and the camera tightened its shot on me. I smiled and waved; I was missing my two front teeth. Mom and Dad broke for a commercial. I blacked out again.

TWENTY-FOUR

Tony

I followed Pace and MacNamara into the interrogation room, my pulse ratcheting up with every step down the sterile hallway. I imagined a scene from a movie, with cinder-block walls and restraints everywhere. I was waiting for someone to shackle my wrists when Pace pushed open a conference room door and ushered us inside. I looked at Bellingham. He raised his eyebrows and gestured toward one of the nondescript chairs around a big, oval conference table.

I sat, then Bellingham did, then Pace and MacNamara arranged themselves across from us, an old-school tripod and ancient video camera aimed directly at me.

"If you don't mind, we'll be recording your confession, Tony."

"Statement," Bellingham snapped.

Pace licked his lips and smiled, but didn't make eye contact. "Right, statement."

"Officer, I expect, and my client deserves, respect from you and your partner. He has not been charged with anything."

Pace opened his mouth, but MacNamara held up a silencing hand, her gaze soft but pinning Bellingham and me. "Of course. Our apologies." She turned to me. "Now, Tony, why don't you go ahead and tell us what you remember about that last conversation you had with Hope?"

TWENTY-FIVE

Hope

I waited for Daniel to kill me.

I waited to die.

But he didn't, and when I woke up, his face was way too close to mine. My whole body ached. I pulled back, shrank into myself, and Daniel actually looked wounded, hurt. I knew I should strike again, but nothing worked. Synapses fired, but nothing responded.

Daniel smiled slowly and spoke in a soft, clipped cadence. "I have something to show you."

He was on hands and knees in front of me, crouching forward like an eager dog, and I could see the bones of his shoulder blades sticking out at the back of his shirt. I could also see that his shirt was stained with splatters of rust, drips of red.

My blood.

I tasted bile in my throat.

Daniel cocked his head, anxious. "Hope?"

I wanted to tell him not to say my name. I wanted to rush

forward, to throttle him and crack every bone in his body, but my head felt like it weighed a thousand pounds and the dull, metallic taste of blood was still heavy in my mouth. I tried to swish my tongue in my mouth, but it felt like I was pushing through cotton.

"Water," I heard myself choke out.

The smile on Daniel's face dropped, and he seemed genuinely concerned. "I'm so sorry. Of course you're thirsty."

My vision was half-blurred and blood tinged, but I could see Daniel push himself off the floor and scramble to a little alcove just off the room we were in. I heard him fumble with something that sounded like dishes, heard water glug into a cup. Daniel came back and crouched in front of me again, then slowly, gingerly even, pressed his palms against my shoulders and slid me to a sitting position. He pressed a plastic cup to my lips, and I could see a grease spot swirl and congeal on the top of the water. My stomach lurched, but my tongue seemed to swell even more, and I gulped when he pressed the cup to my lip and tipped it forward. Water rushed down my throat, my chin, and soaked the front of my shirt.

"Oh," Daniel said, stunned. He looked away. "Sorry about that."

I didn't know what he was apologizing for, but wildly, in my head, I know it was not for having kidnapped me, hog-tying me, and dumping me on the filthy wooden floor. I knew it was probably for some lunacy like dripping water on my T-shirt, and the absurdity of the situation hit me square in the chest. A bubble of laughter started there. I tried to wrestle it down, but it was gurgling in my throat, and I could feel the goofy smile spread across my lips that were cracked and broken, held together with dried blood and saliva.

I was laughing.

Daniel smiled, amused or thrilled, then started laughing too. "I knew I could make you happy if you'd just give me half the chance."

The terrifying implications of that statement didn't register. Nothing did, except the laughter, and I kept going on like a hysterical hyena.

"I have something to show you," Daniel said again. "I almost forgot. Come on." He pushed himself to his feet and beckoned over his shoulder as if I could move at all under my own free will. Then he slapped his forehead and said, "Oh, let me help you!" as though he was some sort of demented 1950s gentleman. He pulled me up, and the knife was there again, rusty and dull, and the laughter was snatched from my chest along with my breath.

I inched my feet backward, felt the rope rubbing into the raw skin on my ankles, and I started to shake. It came from somewhere deep in my center, a terror that I couldn't handle, that I couldn't control, and I could feel the sweat roll off me in waves, could smell the acrid stench of fear—my own.

Daniel looked at the knife. "Oh no. This?" He poked at it as though it were a benign object like a hunk of cotton or an ice cream cone. "I'm just going to…" And he flicked the edge of the blade across the length of rope.

My legs were free.

The gashes in my ankle stung when the rope fell away and a fresh burst of oxygen hit.

I should run. I should kick.

But Daniel jabbed his shoulder into my belly and had me in an awkward bear hug, my calves and thighs pinned against his body, my feet hanging bare and useless between his legs. My arms are still pinned to my sides, and when I tried to squirm, the rope there rubbed against my T-shirt, the fabric burning my skin.

"You're going to love this," he said as he shuffled forward, carrying me. "I did it just for you."

My head whipped around as he shuffle-walked, carrying me. I tried to take in every inch of the tiny house, making mental notes of escape routes and what could be used as weapons. There really was nothing: A threadbare couch. A giant spool coffee table. A flimsy lamp, a thousand-pound television set with a picture that broke into static every few seconds. A wood-paneled hallway with nothing on the walls.

"Bathroom." I suddenly muttered.

It was across the hall from where we stopped; I could just see it through the wedge of an open door. There was a medicine cabinet I was sure I could wrench off the wall, a mirror that would be easy enough to crack, its shards to use like knives. I could just see the edge of a dingy shower curtain, gross, but probably slick enough to use for strangulation. Hell, the toilet seat, the toilet tank lid. I could wriggle through the tiny, high window or scream like bloody mad. There could be toiletries that would burn eyes, a metal nail file for jabbing…

"Can I use the restroom, please?"

Daniel looked at me and then into the bathroom, his eyes sweeping my cache of possible weapons. "Don't you want to see my surprise?"

I was very, very sure I did not.

"I really have to go." I furrowed my brows and tried to look small and helpless.

Daniel shrugged and smiled. "Then I guess we have to go."

"We?"

He let me down on the floor but kept a firm, steady hold on my arm, shuffling me over the torn linoleum.

"Uh, I can't really…" I kind of wriggled to show that I'd need to be untied. "And can I have a little privacy, please?" I forced a blush into my cheeks.

Daniel blinked at me and once again seemed to survey the interior of the bathroom. I opened my eyes wide, hoping the look was innocent and forthright.

"You'll have to leave the door open."

"Oh." I bit my bottom lip. "Daniel, I can't… I-I don't even know you. That would be so embarrassing." I could feel my heart slamming against my chest, my breath coming in fast little pulses. *This could be my way out. This could be my only chance to escape.*

"I just have to pee, I promise," I said sweetly. "You can stand right outside the door. I'll just be a minute. Please?" I cocked my head and licked my lips. It was a champion move on dates; I hoped Daniel was as gullible.

"Okay, sure, Hope. I trust you." He went to work untying the rope that pinned my arms down, and I prayed he couldn't hear my clattering heart, that he couldn't feel the relief that rolled off me. I chewed the inside of my cheek while he worked, anything to keep my nerves steady, since with every centimeter the ropes loosened, I wanted to run.

When I was fully untied, Daniel caged me in the hallway, an arm on either side of the bathroom doorjamb. I backed in and tried to close the door nonchalantly, though everything inside me told me to slam it as hard as possible, told me to mash that door so hard it would fly off the hinges and bash the bastard in the face. I went to lock the door, but Daniel had the knob in his hand and pressed the door open two inches.

"Don't lock it."

"Got it," I said, pulling the door closed a slight bit more forcefully. "Just one second."

I really did have to pee, but I didn't dare. The second the door clicked shut, I spun, yanked open that medicine cabinet, and planned my escape.

TWENTY-SIX

Tony

I finished my story—again—while Pace stared at me and MacNamara took notes. I tried to look nonchalant, but my eyes kept going to the video camera, to the stupid red light that flashed, letting me know that everything I was saying was being recorded.

Again.

We lapsed into silence—an incredibly uncomfortable silence—and I opened my mouth and rushed to fill the silence, but Bellingham put his hand on my arm and shot me a stern look.

"Any more questions?"

Pace and MacNamara exchange a look, and I had a vague flashback to some *Law and Order* episode. I wondered if they were going to do some sort of good cop/bad cop routine. And then I remembered that this was my life, not some television show.

"So why don't you tell us about the Internet?" Pace said.

I swallowed a ball of white-hot heat. "Excuse me?"

MacNamara produced a file folder, opened it, and started reading. "Instagram. Twitter. Snapchat."

Social media. I started to relax.

"Hope was on everything."

I nodded slowly.

"Tinder, Cupid Cat. She even signed herself up for something called Bangbook." MacNamara looked up at me, and I shifted. "And for the Desert Storm Survival chat room. Some interesting choices for a high school girl, don't you think?"

"I don't know," I said.

Bellingham blew out a dramatic sigh. "Are you going somewhere with this, officer?"

"Hope's information was everywhere online. And prior to her going missing, she was complaining about it. Do you have anything to say about that, Tony?"

I thought of that final screen: *Share Location?* Saw Hope's GPS coordinates line up in my head before they were broadcast out to the world, to any idiot with a computer and an Internet connection. I had put a target on Hope's back.

"I don't think Hope is really missing—" I said quickly.

"We have nothing further." Bellingham clipped the end of my statement, but MacNamara was already on me.

"And where do you think Hope is?"

I shook my head and clasped my hands in my lap. "I don't know, but her friend Everly even said…"

The legs of Bellingham's chair scraped loudly against the floor as he quickly stood up and grabbed my arm. "Are we done here?"

"Who exactly is Everly, Tony?" Pace wanted to know.

"Everly Byer," I supplied, avoiding Bellingham's death glare. "She goes to our school. She's right outside." I pointed, like she would mysteriously appear through the wall.

"Isn't she the one who came to visit you?" Pace asked calmly.

I could feel myself go white, could feel the saliva go sour in my mouth. "She just stopped by. She just came by on her own."

There was a hint of a smile on Pace's face, and I didn't like it.

"And she's a good friend of Hope's?"

I thought of Everly sitting at my kitchen table, of the way her eyes were hard and steel blue when she talked about Hope, and I started to feel uneasy. "Well…yeah. I mean, they were."

"And she has some ideas about where Hope may have gone?" It was MacNamara then, her voice soft and motherly, encouraging even. I stared at my shoes.

"You should talk to her maybe." I thought of Everly's lips then, pressed against mine, eager, insistent, surprising. I felt the heat cross my cheeks, and I knew I was blushing. I stared harder at my shoes, hoping no one would notice, hoping the earth would split open and swallow me up, or split open and spit Hope back out.

* * *

Most of the crowds had dispersed by the time I was done. I scanned the group that was left, looking for Everly, but stopped when Bellingham clapped a hand on my shoulder and growled in my ear.

"Next time, I do all the talking."

I nodded dumbly, half listening, half wondering if Pace and

MacNamara had sent someone out to collect Everly. Was she giving her statement right now?

Bellingham kept hold of my arm, and my parents flanked me on either side. I walked like a robot, head down, trying to focus on putting one foot in front of the other, nothing else. But I heard them.

"Mr. Gardner, Mr. Gardner, are you officially a suspect in this case?"

"Mr. Gardner, did you a give a statement to the police?"

"Mr. Gardner! Mr. Gardner!"

"Tony!"

I whipped around, staring at these strangers who knew my name. They leered. They shoved their microphones forward.

A heavyset man in a Channel 7 windbreaker stepped in front of us, arm extended, microphone an inch from my nose.

"Where's Hope?" he asked. "Tony, where's Hope?"

TWENTY-SEVEN

Hope

I felt like I was going to pass out.

There were two rusty shelves in the medicine cabinet, a bottle of aspirin that looked like it had been there as long as I'd been alive, and a pair of tweezers rusted shut. I shoved the tweezers in my pocket and tried until sweat beaded my upper lip to remove either one of the shelves. They didn't budge.

Daniel knocked heavily on the door. "Are you okay in there?"

"Uh-huh." It came out as kind of an inelegant grunt. "Just one sec."

If I stood on my tiptoes, the edges of my fingertips would just brush the bottom of the stupid window. The glass was frosted and thick, the kind that wouldn't shatter. I knew because I tried, fake coughing as my fist hit the edge of the glass. I punched until my palm felt raw, until heat raged from my shoulder to wrist.

"Hope?"

Daniel tried the knob, and I sprang from the window and

flushed the toilet, frantically looking for something else to try. I climbed on the lip of the tub, years of grime slick under my feet. I tugged at the shower curtain, the cheap vinyl ripping easily, silently—uselessly. I grabbed the curtain rod, my shoulders jarring, but it was firmly rusted into the place. Hopeless tears pricked at my eyes as I looked for something, anything: shampoo to burn his eyes. A straight razor. Even a loofah with some heft.

There was nothing.

My stomach was churning. Sweat dripped from my forehead, stinging as it fell into my eyes.

"Hope, open the door." Daniel's voice was even but sharp.

"I'm not done yet."

"Open. The. Door."

I clawed at the window, the skin on my fingertips tearing as I gripped, swore, prayed. Bloody prints streaked through the inch-thick dirt on the window.

"Hope!"

Daniel was furiously working the knob, the door shaking on flimsy hinges. My heart slammed against my chest as I heard his full body weight hitting the frame. The door seemed to bow, and I couldn't tell if tears or sweat were clouding my vision.

"Open this door right now, or I'm coming in!"

I went for the medicine cabinet again, pressed a foot against the wall, slugged my body weight backward, but nothing happened. The damn thing was bolted into place. My heart continued to slam; my breath was ragged as the blood coursed through my veins.

But Daniel had gone quiet.

I took two tentative steps and leaned my ear toward the door. "Hello?" I whispered.

Nothing, but the *thud-thud-thud* of my heart, strangling my lungs, tightening in my throat.

"Open the fucking door, Hope!"

I scrambled backward into the pit of the bathroom. My feet tried to find purchase, my bloody, broken fingers scrabbling over the slick linoleum floor.

I heard the first piece of wood splinter—loud, sharp, like bones breaking.

"Hope!"

I yanked the top off the toilet tank as the door imploded. Daniel, red faced and furious, was standing in the splinters, an ax swinging low by his side.

"Come here, Hope."

I crouched by the toilet, every muscle in my body coiled and on high alert, the lactic acid pulsing and aching. My bloody fingers were gripping the heavy porcelain top of the toilet tank.

"Come and get me, motherfucker."

Daniel's eyes rolled over me, a mix of rage, amusement, and confusion flittering through.

"What are you doing?" he asked.

I didn't answer, panting, teeth gritted.

"You promised you would just be a second."

I didn't lose my grip on the toilet tank lid even as sweat lined my palms. "I'm sorry. I'm not into keeping promises to psychopaths."

Daniel looked genuinely confused for the millisecond I gave

him before I leaped forward, throwing my weight toward my arms, toward the toilet tank lid that I swung over my left shoulder. I heard it make contact, a loud, metallic clank bookended by a thunderous grunt. I didn't stick around to see what I'd hit. I bounded across the bathroom floor and vaulted over Daniel, feeling the sticky linoleum floor bruise the ball of my foot as I went.

I cleared Daniel.

I cleared the remains of the bathroom door. I didn't stop when a shard of wood stood up and lanced through the back of my heel. I dropped the toilet tank lid and let the pain and blood at my foot propel me through the living room with the ancient, lined TV and into the dining room, where I could still hear the studio audience applauding something darling my parents had said to each other.

Rage burned in my chest.

I heard Daniel moan, heard him lurch.

Found the front door.

I was commanding my fingers to work, to grab hold of the chain lock that seemed minuscule in my fumbling fingers.

"Hope!" Daniel screamed my name, and tears poured from my eyes. I had my hand on the doorknob, trying to get a grip even though my palms were sweating.

It was locked.

I stared at the door incredulously, like I'd expected something else. Bile itched at the back of my throat as I heard Daniel push himself up from the hall and thump against the walls as he came toward me. He was fast, faster than he should have been. I could see him out of the corner of my eye, see that his hair was messed up, see that I left a four-inch gash over his left eyebrow. It looked raw and purple and angry, blood deeply red and thick dribbling over his eyebrow. He used a fist to wipe it away, and the blood swirled in the white of his eye.

"Don't even try it, Hope."

My eyes went to the door, to the neat row of locks spaced up the jamb.

"Hope." Daniel took a slow step toward me.

My fingers felt numb as I yanked the first chain free, my other hand working the paralyzed knob. I pulled it uselessly, then worked the first deadbolt free, then the second. I glanced over my shoulder to where Daniel should have been, but he wasn't there. I stopped for a heartbeat, my stomach going to liquid.

"There's nowhere to run, Hope."

He was closer then, supremely, terrifyingly calm while the panic ratcheted up in my chest, my breath coming out a strangled sob.

One more.

"Hope!"

I ignored Daniel, my lips pursed as the final deadbolt slipped free and opened with a click. I yanked open the front door, squinting at the sunlight and breathing in a big gulp of redwood air. I didn't bother to look over my shoulder. I didn't bother to look for shoes. I was over the threshold when the doorjamb exploded, pieces of wood splintering and showering my hair, the back of my neck.

I smelled the gunpowder.

I kept running.

I didn't know how much ground I'd covered, but my feet were

ripped raw. My thighs were burning, my calves tightening like fists with every step I took, but I wouldn't stop. My heart slammed against my rib cage, and my throat was blistered dry, my lips cracked. I wanted to stop. I wanted to stop and collapse and fall and be home in my room, but I couldn't because I didn't know where Daniel was. I didn't know how close he was.

I didn't even know where I was.

I doubled over when the cramp overwhelmed me, a screaming pain from the base of my ribs tearing up through my lungs, stabbing my throat. My whole body heaved, my breath, hot and dry, was choking me, and my stomach constricted. I gagged, dry heaved, was forced to stop. I stumbled over my own feet, could see the mud and blood caked between my toes before I heaved again and my eyes clouded over with tears.

I took a deep breath, the smell of pine and dirt overwhelming me, the cool rush of forest air whipping over my teeth, past my parched tongue.

I had to stop. I couldn't keep running. Had to stop at least for a second.

The ground cracked.

Gunfire.

I needed to run, but my knees locked and my breath clamped tight in my throat. Instead I pitched forward, dropped to my belly. I dug the pads of my fingers into the ground, yanking up dry grass and dirt, feeling pebbles dig themselves under my fingernails as I pulled my whole body forward, inch by painful, tearing inch.

Another gunshot.

That one sent a round of crows cawing and seemed to shake every needle off the pine trees around me. I had to move. I had to hide. Daniel was near.

TWENTY-EIGHT

Tony

Bellingham was silent on the car ride home. My parents were quiet when they walked in the front door. Even Alice didn't do much more than glance at me over the rim of her Happy Meal cup when I sat down at the table. The television was on again, another endless loop of voiceless heads nodding and looking upset while Hope's picture flashed in the background. I sat up straighter when the picture of Hope dissolved and there was someone else there: Everly. She was standing on the steps of the school with one of the news reporters.

I leaned over and clicked the volume on.

"This is Everly Byer, and you are…"

Everly looked gorgeous, model ready in tight jeans and a slim-fitting sweater. Her hair was blonder than ever, brushed into big, soft waves; her eyes were more piercing, bluer than I had ever seen. She looked less like herself, less like the girl who had railed against Hope in my kitchen the other night.

She looked like Hope.

"Hope is my best friend," Everly said, expertly commandeering the anchorman's microphone. "I've organized this vigil tonight with Bruce and Becky"—she paused so the cameraman could flash on Bruce and Becky—"because we *are* going to bring you home, Hope. We'll never stop looking for you." Her voice cracked, her eyes going from that icy blue to glossy, misted.

"Everly, what do you think happened to your friend? There is some speculation that Hope possibly ran away."

I had to give Everly credit. She was nearly flawless. Her eyes widened, the tears suspended on ultra-long lashes as she shook her head slowly from side to side, her blond curls swishing.

I sucked in a breath, waiting. Everly would tell the truth. Everly was on my side. She would let the world know—Pace, MacNamara—she would let them all know that Hope had staged the whole thing.

"Hope would never do that to us. She knows how much we all love her. I know that she would reach out if she could. Hope…" Everly's voice trembled, and she turned her blue eyes directly to the camera, imploringly. "Please, whoever has Hope, please just don't hurt her. Let her go. No questions asked. We just want Hope home."

I felt my jaw tighten, my molars rubbing together. *What?*

"So you don't believe there is any truth to the speculation that Hope may have left on her own accord?"

I thought Everly's eyes would pop out of her head. "No, of course not." She shuddered. "Why would someone even do that?"

The news anchor shrugged slightly. "Attention, maybe?"

Everly shook her head. "Not Hope. Hope wasn't like that. Isn't like that," she hurriedly corrected herself, then shoved a fistful of white candles into the shot. "That's why I've organized tonight's vigil. Here, at the school. Everyone is welcome." She offered a demure yet dazzling smile.

I flicked the channel—a baseball game, an ad for creamer, then Bruce and Becky on Channel 7.

"…miss you, Hope." Bruce was in mid-plea, Becky holding on to his arm, her fingers spidered against his skin. "Please, if you have any information regarding Hope's whereabouts, call the number on the screen."

A number and website were superimposed over a black-and-white photo of Hope. She was wearing a white gown and looking sweet and angelic. My throat tightened.

Hope was missing, but she was everywhere.

The camera snapped back to Bruce and Becky. Becky leaned forward, her eyes wide and suitably dewy, but still camera ready. "A candlelight vigil will be held tonight at nine p.m. We will be assembling on the steps of the Florence High School library and walking over to August Woods."

Bruce glanced at Becky and squeezed her knee. "August Woods is one of Hope's favorite places. She loves to meditate in nature."

I snort laughed. My parents whipped to face me, and even Alice went wide-eyed.

"I'm sorry," I said, clapping a hand over my mouth. "I'm sorry, but that's just ridiculous. Hope never meditated. And if she were ever to start, it sure as heck wouldn't happen in August Woods

Park. She always said it was full of drunks and degenerates. And the closest she got to nature was walking on the field after cheerleading practice. Seriously, a ladybug landed on her sock, and she had her entire outfit sent out for dry cleaning."

My parents looked at me stiffly, not laughing. My mother looked horrified, my father unreadable.

"Guys, I'm just saying. I mean, she was…"

My mother swallowed hard and scooped Alice onto her hip. "Let's go get your bath, baby."

"Dad?"

My dad rooted through the fridge, got himself a beer, and took a long, slow pull. He was a beer-during-football kind of guy. He was also not the kind of guy who would avoid his son, but that's what he did now. He avoided my eyes, gave me a wide berth, and disappeared into the garage. My parents' silent accusation clung to me and weighted me down.

Share Location?

If they were ever going to be able to look at me again, I had to end this. I had to come clean. I had to find Hope.

I grabbed my car keys, slid into my windbreaker, and stalked out the front door.

TWENTY-NINE

Hope

Every step I took into the forest sent a new shiver down my spine. The temperature dropped, and another dark fingerprint of night clouded my vision. I tried to remember everything I had learned in self-defense classes, tried to recall everything I'd seen characters do in survival-type situations. I cocked my head and listened for civilization—cars on a road, hikers calling out to each other—but there was only silence.

The quiet was all encompassing. Deafening. Even the sounds of nature were mute. There was no breeze, no rustling leaves or crackling twigs. For that I should have been grateful, but all I could think about was being alone—alone with Daniel somewhere out here. I tried to get my bearings, racking my brain for any clue that would tell me which direction I should be going, but there was nothing. To my left, the trees were huge, heavy branches thick with pine needles, some scraping the ground. The tree trunks were massive, some burned out, some so choked with thorny vines that

I couldn't see where one ended and the other began, but I knew I couldn't go through them.

To my right, the tree trunks were thinner but the forest was denser, just inches between some trees with the occasional boulder interspersed, a thick blanket of moss covering everything. I shrunk into my T-shirt, wishing I still had my hoodie and my shoes, but the thought of Daniel, of going back to that house—to his weird, plaintive eyes and flat mouth—made my blood run cold. I had to keep going, to keep walking. I had to make a decision, to pick a direction and just go. But when I heard the twig breaking behind me, I was paralyzed.

I stopped, praying for that once-deafening silence, but suddenly there was noise everywhere: Blue jays cawing. Something small scrabbling through the pine needles and dry brush. The thud of my heart. The rush of my blood.

He'll hear me.

I didn't dare breathe, the sound a ragged tear through my lungs, but my lungs constricted and burned, and I let out a half groan, half breath.

He's on to me for sure.

I dug my toes into the wet ground and pushed off, hands fisted, legs pumping, running again. Pine needles were slapping at my bare skin and felt like they were slicing across my arms.

There!

Through the trees. A snatch of color zipping by.

A car.

My heart swelled and slammed against my rib cage.

There was a road up ahead.

I couldn't hear the motors, the tires on the road, but I knew they were there. They *had to be there.* Up ahead, a little farther. There was a clearing, and I dropped to my knees, crouching down like an animal and looking wildly around. I paused, listening for Daniel. Leaves breaking, twigs cracking, footsteps across the soft, moss-covered earth?

Nothing.

I pushed myself forward on hands and knees. I could feel twigs and tiny rocks pressing against my knees, cutting into my palms, but I didn't care. I left a trail of blood. I kept pressing on. It seemed to take forever, but finally I was at the edge of road. I felt like I could breathe for the first time.

The first car whizzed by and I wasn't ready for it, but the breeze it created—a thick, hot wind twinged with cold from the night air—slapped my face, and I laughed.

I was saved.

I pushed myself to standing, stumbled to the middle of the road. The blacktop was still vaguely warm on the bottoms of my feet, and I waved my arms over my head in the darkness. My heart was still thundering.

I kept waving.

No one was coming.

There were no streetlights, and the dark that was just a mild smudge was closing in, was squeezing out every inch of daylight. I could feel my feet on the concrete. I could feel the cold settling into my fingertips.

But I couldn't see anything.

I couldn't hear anything.

The air left my lungs. My entire body deflated, and I crumbled to my knees and rolled to my side, trying to absorb every bit of the cement's heat into my body. I was shivering now, and crying.

No one was coming. I was all alone.

THIRTY

Tony

There must have been a thousand cars in the school parking lot. Every spot was taken, and people had commandeered the pockmarked back forty, making it into an overflow lot. I edged my car into the only bare stretch of lawn I could find, glad that there was a fire lane and frontage road for a quick escape. I put my hood up and hunkered down in the dark, glancing around surreptitiously, but trying to hang back and let the darkness shroud me. I didn't want to be noticed. Not here. Not at Hope's candlelight vigil.

A group of girls were huddled in front of me, pushing their candles together. I didn't recognize the girls until someone struck a match. Then I saw Everly, her lips drawn, the hard planes of her face illuminated in the orange-yellow light. She saw me and smiled. The other girls turned then and noticed me too. They bristled.

"What's he doing here?" I heard one say.

"I think it's sweet. He still cares for Hope," Everly said.

"He's the reason Hope's missing."

Ice water shot through my veins.

I ignored the girls and kept walking.

If there were a thousand cars in the parking lot, there were two thousand people gathered on the steps of the school library. I recognized most of them from school, but there were also adults from town, people who were looking around incredulous, like they were at some sort of show, and others who clamored close to Bruce and Becky and the Channel 7 camera crew. There were flowers flanking the steps—big, ugly arrangements—and a banner stretched across. Pictures of Hope. Reporters. News anchors. Uniformed police officers. Pace. MacNamara.

If everyone in the police department was here, I wondered, was there anyone out there looking for Hope?

"Hey." Everly broke away from her clutch of girls and handed me a candle rolled in a paper plate. "Want me to light you?"

I took the candle from her and nodded silently. She cupped her hand over the wick and struck a match.

"I'm surprised that you're here."

"I'm a little surprised that you're here too," I told her.

"Why would you say that?"

I leaned closer, dropping my voice to a whisper because I could see that we were being watched. "Because of what you said."

Everly raised her brows. "What I said?"

"About Hope staging this whole thing. You said that to me, but I saw the news today, Everly. And this whole vigil?"

She blinked, wide-eyed, doing a great rendition of I-don't-know-what-you're-talking-about. Then she looked over each shoulder, clamped a hand on my arm, and dragged me away from the crowd, then threaded her arms in front of her chest.

"Shut up about that, will you?" she hissed.

"Shut up about what?"

"Of course I wasn't going to tell the news people that I think Hope staged this whole thing. What would they think?"

"Maybe they would think I wasn't a suspect and get the heck off my lawn."

Everly narrowed her eyes, and I went palms up. "Look, I don't know what you're doing. I don't know why you're doing this since we both think that Hope is out there laughing her ass off at all of this. But you have to go to the police. Please, Everly, you have to. Tell them what you told me."

Everly rolled her eyes. "I'm doing this vigil to bring Hope home."

"Great."

"I figured she'd see all of this and make a grand appearance. Then, you know, problem solved." Her smile was a little too bright, a little too loose.

"Do you know something else about Hope, Everly?"

Everly kept smiling but held it a beat too long, and gooseflesh pricked my arms. Could she have something do with Hope's disappearance?

"Everly?"

"Hope is one of my best friends, Tony. I don't know what you want me to say." She was talking too loud now, taking a sharp step away from me. "Now if you'll excuse me, I have to go pass out these candles."

"Hey, is this goon bothering you?" Rustin came over Everly's left shoulder, and she seemed to shrink into him. His lip was still slightly swollen, and there was a half-inch cut under his right eye.

"We were just talking." I couldn't take my eyes off the damage to Rustin's face. I was both ashamed and intrigued.

"You shouldn't be here, dude."

Anger bubbled in my chest. "*You* shouldn't be here, dude. You know where Hope is."

Another girl from Everly's gaggle stepped into the fray. She looked at Rustin and then at me, her eyes narrowing. "What's *he* doing here?"

"I have as much right to be here as anyone else." I paused, my mouth dry. "I care about Hope too."

Rustin snorted. "You care about saving your own ass."

"Everyone, everyone?" Everly was at the stop of the stairs now, holding a microphone that was giving off bad reverb. Bruce and Becky were at her side, as well as the chief of police. In front of them was the ever-present camera crew, and I could see Bruce and Becky reflected in the cameraman's feedback, their perfect features illuminated by their lit Bring Hope Home candles.

Everly broke into a story about her and Hope's friendship, and my stomach turned as I glanced at the faces all around me. They were rapt, paying firm attention, some with silent tears flowing down their cheeks. Even Pace and MacNamara were standing still, staring. But no one was looking for Hope. It was all a beautiful show with tears and candlelight and soft, white roses—but no one was out looking for Hope. If she staged this, she was having a good laugh. If she didn't, she was out there somewhere, alone, and no one was looking for her.

I blew out my candle and tossed it in the trash on my way to the car.

THIRTY-ONE

Hope

At first, I couldn't distinguish the rumble, but then it came through me, louder, harder. Started in my hip. In my shoulder. Vibrated up the side of my leg and along my spine until my teeth were almost chattering. A car engine.

I vaulted off the darkened street, lurching to the side enough to be seen but not hit. I was waving frantically, even as every muscle in my body ached in protest. I wanted to sleep, but I needed to get out of here. Then, finally, I saw it in the distance: two yellow orbs. One wobbled slightly to the left. Headlights.

I was saved.

If I could have smiled, I would have. If I had anything left in me, I would have laughed. Instead I just stood there, spread-eagle, arms over my head, sucking in great lungfuls of air and letting the tears roll over my cheeks.

The headlights crept closer.

The vibration of the engine on the concrete tickled my bare

feet, zoomed up my calves, and sent an electric, life-giving zing throughout my body.

Saved.

The driver saw me.

My whole body lightened.

The car began to slow, to veer to the side.

I used everything I had left inside to stumble ahead, to force my legs to move, to pump forward, jogging to meet the truck.

"Oh God, thank you so much! Oh my God, thank you!" I knew there was snot dribbling down my chin, but I didn't care. I could barely see through the tears.

The automatic door locks clicked, and I got the door open, letting the warmth of the car's interior wash over me.

"I need to get out of here! He's still out there, and he's after me and he's—"

"*Shh, shh* now. *Shh.* You're safe now, Hope."

Daniel had my arm before I could respond, his fingers closing around my bare skin. I just stared at those carefully manicured fingernails gripping me, incredulous. He began to pull me into the cab.

"I'll always find you, Hope. I'm always watching you, your friends." He smiled. "It was meant to be."

Blood pulsed through my veins and throbbed in my temples. I punched out with my free hand, twisting until I thought my arm might break. "Let me go, let me go!"

All at once, Daniel shoved the car into park and lurched halfway over the seat, grabbing me in a rib-crushing bear hug. I kicked out, feeling the flesh of my feet and toes dig into the asphalt, feeling tiny pieces of gravel ripping into my skin. My shin hit the side of the car. I twisted and flopped like a caught fish, clawing my fingers, digging at everything I could find: Daniel's skin, his hair, the cheap vinyl dashboard.

"What are you doing? Stop that!"

I gripped at whatever I could, throwing handfuls of stuff out the open passenger-side door: a receipt, a water bottle, a chunk of my own hair.

If Daniel was going to remove me from this stupid spot on the road, I was going to make sure the police knew I had been there.

"Hope, stop!"

Fire raged through me. When Daniel moved to shove me into the seat, to restrain me or buckle me, or whatever he was trying to do, I freed my hand and went right to his hat, grabbing it and a handful of hair.

"What are you—"

I yanked.

I felt the sickening, satisfying tug of hair, then felt it break.

"*Oooowwww!*"

I tossed the hat through the open door, while Daniel's hands pressed against his head. I was free again.

I was out of the car, on the ground, scrabbling through the litter of evidence I had managed to toss. But Daniel was on top of me. This time, there were no kind words. This time, there was no struggle.

There was a pinprick. Something at the base of my neck, and suddenly, my limbs were heavy, and I wasn't sure if I was closing my eyes. I told myself, warned myself, begged myself not to close my eyes, but the blackness was closing in on me anyway. The last thing I saw was Daniel on his feet, but leaning over me, hands on his knees, his expression drawn, almost sad.

"It shouldn't have had to be this way, Hope. I really, really didn't want to do that."

I wanted to respond, but my lips were swollen, my tongue stuck to the roof of my mouth. I felt like I was melting into the asphalt. I felt like I should say good-bye.

I felt like I was already dead.

THIRTY-TWO

Tony

I wanted to floor it, to tear out of the school parking lot, but I crept out achingly slowly as the crowd continued to grow, their candles burning en masse. They had piped in some sappy music, and people were crying outright now. I could see their red faces and shoulders heaving even as I drove through the lot. Bette Midler songs and candles weren't going to bring Hope home.

I was going to bring her home.

I went on instinct, without thinking, coasting onto the freeway at seventy-five. I passed the exit to Hope's house, passed the beach one, and followed the exit Rustin took the day I followed him. It dropped me at the edge of a blink-and-you'll-miss-it mountain town, a single two-lane highway with a series of rustic-looking buildings lining one side: An old-timey hardware store. A sundries shop, a pancake house, a Gas 'N' Go, a bar. The other side of the street was dense with forest, huge redwoods yawning into the ever-darkening night.

I rolled up my windows and pumped the heat, continuing on the road until it came to a vee. One fork pointed toward a resort town called Twin Pines; the other dipped down into the forest. I took the forest road and kicked on my high beams. There were no houses. There was no cluster of buildings, no Hope sneering from the side of the road.

I drove about six miles, licking deeper into the forest, feeling more and more deflated.

Hope could be anywhere.

I drove a few more miles and passed a hundred more trees that all looked exactly the same until I came to a turnout. A lone streetlight blinked ominously on the side of the road, and I almost laughed at the absurdity, at the stereotype of one flickering light on a desolate road while the poor sap main character looked in vain for his lost love. I turned around with a screech, leaving the mess of garbage and a lost baseball cap rolling on the side of the road, and headed home.

THIRTY-THREE

Hope

I woke up as if from drowning, my head breaking through the surface of sleep. I gasped, trying to get my lungs to work. There was a hideously sweet taste in my mouth, caked at the corners of my lips. Once the fuzz dissipated, I blinked: a kitchen.

Vaguely familiar.

Voices.

"And once again, our daughter, Hope!"

Swell of applause. Morning-show music.

I couldn't stop the sob that ripped through my mouth. There was a clattering, then Daniel dropped down to his knees beside me. "Ooh, ooh, don't do that!" He used a rough hand to wipe the tears from my eyes. I struggled away from him at first, but the fight left me. This was my life now. Flopping like a half-dead fish on some filthy kitchen floor. Daniel would kill me—if not now, soon.

But his eyes were soft.

Concerned, even.

He used a pinkie finger to wipe something crusted at the corner of my mouth. He examined it and so did I: bright pink. He smiled, pushed his finger past his lips, and sucked on it. I gagged.

"It's frosting," he said with a shy grin. "Like from a birthday cake."

My stomach roiled.

"You were very upset, and I was afraid you were going to hurt yourself so I had to"—his milky eyes traveled away from me—"subdue you. I'm really sorry, and I hope I never have to do that again."

I gestured toward the zip ties around my wrists. "I'm still subdued."

"Right now, I'm not sure if I can trust you. You ran away." His nostrils flared with a tiny ripple of anger. "You shouldn't have run."

I looked away, a lump thick in my throat, my eyes hot with tears. I should have run further. I shouldn't have stopped running until I was home, until I was out of this hellhole, away from this forest. I should have—

"Your feet were hurt."

Daniel put his hand on my heel, and I glanced down and saw that he had wrapped my bare feet in gauze.

"You could have really hurt yourself." He smiled, and I bit down bile. "But you're safe now. And we can start over. Hi there, Hope. My name is Daniel." He pushed his hat aside, and I saw the gash I had inflicted. The wound was now cleaned and dressed, and I wondered how long I had been out.

"You weren't out that long," Daniel said, and the idea that he could be reading my mind slithered around my neck and made my blood run cold. "Long enough."

"What did you to do me?"

"Nothing that has lasting effects." He shrugged and smiled again.

"So you drugged me?"

His eyes went hard, dark. His lower lip curled into a snarl. "You made me. I did what I had to do. You wouldn't listen. You aren't listening." He licked his lips. "We're going to be very happy together, Hope. You'll see. I'm going to take you away from all that." Daniel gestured over his shoulder, back to the television with the cracked picture, with my parents breaking into one of their many morning-show banter routines. This time, I was an infant, bouncing on my mother's knee, my bald head wrapped in a crocheted pink headband as I clapped my fat, little baby hands and showed off a toothless smile.

"Why do you have that on?"

"Because I want you to see how bad they were. I want you to see how good you're going to have it." Daniel rubbed his hands together. "We're going to be very happy together."

"I'm not staying here with you. I'm not going to be with you."

Daniel slid his index finger along the plastic zip tie, and I wanted to die. I tried to go slack, to hide the fact that his touch sparked any reaction, but he had that creepy, faraway smile on his face.

"We're going to be so happy."

My body started to shake. I gritted my teeth against it, clamped my eyes shut hard, willed my ears to stop taking in sound.

"So, so happy." He grabbed my chin between his thumb and index finger. "You're going to fall in love with me. You'll see. Just the way I fell in love with you."

He smoothed my hair over my forehead, his touch disconcertingly gentle, and I couldn't stop the tremor that rolled through my body. Daniel's eyebrows went up.

"Are you cold, Hope?"

My lungs constricted, and I was paralyzed, my eyes wide as I watched his fingers go to the first button of his shirt, then the second. Every synapse was firing inside me, my brain screaming at me to run, fight, kick out, move, but all I could do was stare in terror as the next button popped open, then the next until he was pulling his shirt tail out from his pants and shimming out of the plaid shirt.

I let out a squeaking half breath when I realized he had a yellowing tank top under his plaid shirt and that was staying on. Daniel lifted me to a sitting position and draped his shirt over my shoulders, the warmth and scent from the fabric that had been so close to his skin overtaking me, making me nauseous and scared. His body heat radiated.

"Isn't that a little better?"

I didn't respond, certain even the most miniscule movement might slice my skin, might let this man's heat and scent bore into me and infect me to the bone.

"It's not polite to ignore a kind gesture." Daniel's words were slow and even. "What do you say?"

I tried to lick my lips and found I had no saliva. "Thank you?" It was a question, my voice a strained whisper.

It satisfied him.

"That's better. Now, I have something to show you." The glee broke out all over his face, his eyes crinkling at the corners, sparkling. His joy scared me. "I've been waiting so long!"

I went limp as Daniel scooped me up, his arms curled around me.

THIRTY-FOUR

Tony

Wake Up the Bay! was being guest hosted by semicelebrities who ribbed each other jovially before immediately going pressed lipped and sad eyed when they returned to the special segment on finding Hope. They interviewed experts, retired cops, Hope's friends, our teachers. There were even two girls who survived and escaped abduction offering words of strength and encouragement to Hope.

But none of them were out there looking for her.

I pulled out my laptop and closed my blinds, feeling every bit like the shifty suspect the media was making me out to be. I pulled down my search history, knowing that I should be deleting everything, that if Bellingham was right and the police wanted to search my house, they would take this laptop. Every search I had done, every time I had entered Hope's information would make me guilty—of what, I wasn't exactly sure, but it didn't matter. I typed anyway, sifting through Hope's messages, looking for RIDETHEWAVE.

After the *Gotcha* message, he hadn't been online. I tried to bait him using Hope's screen name.

No response.

I waited, paced. Listened to my heart thud in my chest.

Why wouldn't he respond to a post from Hope?

I tried to swallow back the inch of fear that crept up, that tiny, niggling bit of knowing that answered my question. He wouldn't respond if he already had her.

* * *

I checked in for my shift at the grocery store, and everyone stopped to look at me. I couldn't be sure, but I thought the overhead Muzak even stopped playing. The baggers stared at me. The other clerks eyed me warily. I knew everyone here. I'd worked here for over a year and shopped here with my mom since I was Alice's age. But everyone stared like I had two heads.

A woman in the checkout line snaked an arm around her toddler's back. An older man stood up a little straighter as if he was protecting the ten-items-or-less line behind him. Then Mr. Anton came out of his office, sweating and nearly sprinting over to me.

"Hey, Mr. Anton."

He grabbed my arm—not hard, but rougher than I expected—and led me back into his office. "Tony… Hey, son, I'm glad you're here."

I pointed idly toward the back room where the shift report was posted. "I'm working today. I'm sorry I'm a few minutes—"

"Actually, we're overstaffed today." He pretended to look

sheepish. "Little mistake on Mrs. Anton's part. Seems she double-scheduled another checker."

I frowned. "Who did she double-schedule? There were only three checkers out there."

Mr. Anton waved at the air. "It's not important. Why don't you go ahead and take the day off?"

He was smiling. It was big and jovial and fake. He took a handkerchief from his back pocket and dabbed at his glistening hairline, even though it couldn't have been more than sixty-five degrees in his meat-locker office.

"You can even take it off with pay. You know, since it was our mistake."

I glanced though the built-in window and scrutinized the check-stand floor. "There are four checkstands and only three checkers." I held up my apron as if it was definitive proof. "And me."

Again, Mr. Anton patted at the air. "Aw, don't worry about us. We're not even that busy. Take the day off. I insist." Another fake smile. Another blot of the forehead. "As a matter of fact, business has been pretty slow. Why don't you take off the rest of the week?"

There were lines at every checkout stand. Carts were clogging the aisles; the produce cart was sparse. Business was booming.

"What's going on, Mr. Anton?"

He held that weird smile for a beat before blowing out a sigh that seemed to deflate his entire body. "Sit down, Tony."

I sat in one of the stained visitor chairs while Mr. Anton flopped down in his desk chair. He steepled his hands and eyed me. "You have to know how much I value you as a worker, Tony. You've been with us well over a year. Never late, picking up other shifts. Customers love you..."

I was bunching up my apron in my lap, trying to wipe the sweat off my palms, but it kept coming. "Yeah, and?"

"It's just this thing." Mr. Anton was working his hands, making weird gestures. "This whole thing with Hope."

I blinked. "That I have nothing to do with."

"Right, right." Mr. Anton pumped his head. "I know that, and you know that."

I sighed. "But no one else does."

"It's not that. Mrs. Anton... I mean, we're both on your side. But some of the customers..."

I looked outside the window where everyone seemed to have forgotten me. Baggers were chatting, grinning, filling sacks with apples and lunch meat. No one was hiding from me. No one was staring at me, wondering if I was going to snap or take a side of beef hostage.

"This is ridiculous. I'm not even a suspect. I was just Hope's ex-boyfriend."

"I know. Oh, I know, Tony. And I know you're a good guy, and I know how much you love her. I know that you wouldn't do anything to harm anyone, let alone a sweetie like Hope. But this is a family business, and our customers are our bread and butter..."

And they don't want a potential murderer ringing up their chuck roast, I wanted to scream.

"You understand."

HANNAH JAYNE

I didn't, but I nodded anyway just to have something to do. "Sure, yeah, I get it."

"Just until all of this blows over. And we can pay you for the rest of your shift." He pulled out a thick calendar and used a pen to count off the days. "It looks like you were scheduled through the end of this week. How about I just write you a check for the remainder…"

I didn't answer because he was already pulling out his ledger, writing out a check.

"So you're firing me."

Mr. Anton looked up, his thick brows knitted. "No, no…not exactly. Just a…uh…like a layoff."

"Until this all blows over."

He didn't look at me, but he bobbed his head in a seminod. "Exactly. Until this all blows over."

I stood when he handed me the check. He eyed me, and we stood like that for a beat. There was something sad in Mr. Anton's eyes, something that told me he was on my side, but then he pressed the check in my hand, glanced out the window, and told me, "If you'd like to come back to clean out your locker after hours, that might be best. Or, you know what? I can do it for you. Drop your things by your house later."

I wagged my head. "No thank you. There's nothing in there anyway." I wouldn't go back in that break room ever again. I wouldn't go back to a place where everyone thought I was guilty.

The only thing left in my work locker anyway was a crystal that Hope gave me. I didn't want it.

I didn't want any reminders of Hope.

196

THIRTY-FIVE

Hope

Daniel carried me down the hall. I avoided looking at the shattered remains of the bathroom door as he set me down carefully—still pinning my arms to my side, holding me so tightly my ribs felt like they were about to implode—in front of a door on the other side of the hall. He had an eerie, weird grin on his face. My throat constricted when Daniel leaned close to me. His breath was sour, too hot.

"I've been waiting to show you this. I've been waiting for so long."

Tears pricked my eyes, but I wouldn't cry. I wouldn't let him see me cry, couldn't give him that satisfaction. Freaks like him got off on seeing girls terrified, and I wouldn't give him that pleasure, even though everything inside me was on high alert, horrified, certain I was about to die. My heart slammed into my chest, and I was suddenly sorry for everything I had ever done, suddenly sorry I had squandered and wasted my life and that I would never see my parents, never see Tony again.

Tony. All this to punish him.

My stomach lurched, and I wished I could throw up.

I wonder what Tony is thinking?

"I hope you like it."

I half hoped Daniel would kill me.

"I did it for you, Hope." He paused and looked at me, his smile almost sweet. Sweet in a creepy, murderous, drag-his-snakelike-tongue-over-his-bottom-lip way.

I didn't bother with an answer.

Daniel pushed the door open and gently urged me forward. I closed my eyes. I knew I was walking to my death, and for once, I didn't want to see it coming. I didn't know what Daniel had in store for me, but I wasn't going to like it, not like the way he wanted me to.

I heard his breath, heard him over my shoulder. He moved closer, and his breath was on my cheek. I could hear him swallow.

"So?" he said slowly. "Do you like it?"

I kept my eyes clamped shut.

"Well?" Daniel tapped my shoulder. I knew the tap was meant to be a gentle one, but it sent shots of pain down my neck and through my rib cage. "Open your eyes," he whispered.

Tears burned behind them.

I licked my Sahara-dry lips and slowly, slowly opened my eyes.

And I was in my bedroom.

THIRTY-SIX

Tony

I called Bellingham from my car while I sat in the grocery store parking lot. I was seething, but I was also embarrassed. Bellingham answered on the first ring.

"Tony!" He sounded happy—jovial, even—and something like hope blossomed inside me.

"Have you heard anything?"

"About what?"

Deflation. "The case."

"No, nothing. Why? Tony, you haven't—"

"I got fired from my job."

"What?"

"Because they think I took Hope. Because they think—"

My mind flashed back to the woman outside the police station, the one holding the handwritten sign: Murderer. People thought Hope was dead, and they thought that I had something to do with it. My pulse ratcheted up, and my heart slammed against my rib cage. Hope could really be in trouble. She could really be... I didn't want to let myself think it, refused to let myself say it. But I saw the blinking cursor.

Share Location?

I swallowed down a mouthful of bile.

Everything was going to be okay. Everything would be fine. Hope was...

"Look, Tony, I'm sorry about your job. You'll find something else. It'll be just fine. And as far as the case goes, you've got nothing to worry about."

I tried to breathe. "I don't?"

"Nah."

I imagined Bellingham leaning back in his slick leather chair while Mirelle sat in front of him, her red nails *tap-tap-tapping* across the keyboard. "Why do you say that?"

"We haven't heard anything yet. At this point with you, no news is good news."

THIRTY-SEVEN

Hope

"What?" I could barely choke out the word as I took in this world—my world, my bedroom, my gray-lavender walls. My silky, deep-plum-colored bedspread. My bookshelves, studded with stuffed animals. My pictures—Mom and Dad, the three of us, my best friends, me in my cheerleading uniform.

They were all here.

My chair was pushed in tightly under my desk, the blond wood pristine, the desktop lined with all my favorite books. All their spines were glistening, brand-new, not a single one broken like they were on my desk at home.

"What is this?" My voice was breathy, small.

"It's home, Hope. It's your home." Daniel smiled and held out his arms, and if I looked around—just glanced—he was right. "I've been waiting…preparing. I did it all for you. It's just perfect, isn't it? Didn't I do good?"

I turned slowly, terrified. Daniel was right—almost. Everything was there. The animals and photos arranged just so, the pillows puffed just the way Mildred did it, but when I looked closer, terror licked at *my* bedspread, *my* bookshelves, *my* paint. My real curtains ware gauzy like these, but mine were always alight because the window was always open. The window here was clamped shut.

The corners of my room were bright, but the corners of this room showed wear, showed a shadowy darkness where the paint color was not quite right. One of the animals was missing a glass eye. There was a deep crack in the side of the desk that had been sanded over and repainted. Suddenly, everything that I knew, that I loved, that made me feel at home in my home was dark and sinister, tainted by horror, by something awful, by Daniel who had taken my life and painstakingly tried to reconstruct it.

"How did you…?" I couldn't finish the thought, and Daniel rushed on.

"I watch you, Hope. I've always watched you, and I paid attention. I couldn't believe my luck when you came out here with that boy. I knew then it was meant to be. You were coming to me. I've been waiting for this for a long, long time. I did it for you. I did it for us."

"How have you been…" I blinked and forced myself to look— to really look, to study—Daniel. "Do I know you?"

He bristled, his smile faltering for a half second. "You don't recognize me."

A lump tightened my throat.

"You never saw me."

"I… I…" I didn't know what to say. I hated this man, despised him. "Who are you?"

His eyes were intent on mine, and I imagined I could see the crazy in them. Then he smiled.

"It doesn't matter who I was. It matters who I am now."

Daniel touched my wrist, his fingers fumbling for my hand. I tried to pull away, but my body was not my own anymore, and everything about me hung limp, forlorn.

"We're going to be so happy together."

This time, I let the tears fall. Daniel cocked his head, wiped a tear from my cheek, and stared at it on his finger for a creepy beat. He smiled again, and I noticed that his teeth were small and uneven, all of them slicing inward like sharks' teeth so every grin took on a sinister, bloodthirsty edge.

"I think I'm going to be sick."

He paled. "Don't do that. But there's a garbage can right there if you need it." He jutted his chin toward a replica of my own trash can at home, and for some reason, this minute, stupid detail was the one that deflated me the most. Something as benign as a garbage can—I don't even know where the one from my room came from, honestly—that he had replicated with painstaking care.

I grabbed the stupid thing in my two hands, leaned over, and retched. When I finished, Daniel took the can from me and handed me a handkerchief. I didn't take it, and he shrugged and pushed the garbage can into the hall.

My eyes darted around him. *If I can just get into the hallway...* But Daniel slowly pulled the door closed, my chance at escape shrinking until the door clicked into place.

"I don't want to do this, but you have to understand that it's only for now. Only until you trust me more." Daniel smiled that weird, should-be-friendly smile and crouched next to the bed. I sucked in a breath as sharp as tacks as he unfurled the chain and held up the viselike clamp on the end of it.

"No." I shrank back, pulled my limbs in to me, and huddled against a wall.

"It's only for a little while until I can trust you."

"You can trust me. I promise."

Daniel cocked his head and pointed to the bandage on his forehead. "I would like to, but I don't think we're there just yet. Don't worry, I won't make it very tight."

My eyes were on the hard metal cuff, on the fat chain links, the three-inch bolt in the floor. "Please, Daniel?"

His voice was stern. "Come on, Hope. I'm not playing." He waggled the chain, and the metal thunked against itself. "Don't make this harder than it has to be."

I didn't react as Daniel darted out a hand and clamped it over my ankle with a sure grip. My fingertips dug into the cheap carpet as he yanked me toward him, slid me closer, my grip useless against his strength. I clamped my eyes shut as he clamped the cuff around my ankle. The cold metal shot goose bumps out along my flesh. I looked at the thing and saw that I was a caged animal. Caught. Trapped.

THIRTY-EIGHT

Tony

The vigil was all over the news now, with Bruce and Becky on every channel, and every channel airing the wide-eyed interview with Everly where she sang Hope's praises and told the world we would never stop looking. There were fund-raisers, interviews... I was pretty sure that, given enough time, a bunch of geriatric rockers would get together and do some sort of Hope-inspired Live Aid sponsored by the Channel 7 news. That's what I was thinking about when my cell phone buzzed.

I glanced at the readout: Everly Byer. I sent it to voice mail, but she buzzed again immediately, then a third time.

"What do you want, Everly?"

"Is this Tony Gardner?" The voice on the other end of the line was even but uncertain. A woman. Not Everly.

"Yes, who's this?"

"My name is Ava Byer. I'm Everly's mother."

I straightened, my skin starting to prickle. "Uh-huh."

Ava Byer cleared her throat, paused, and cleared her throat again.

"Mrs. Byer?"

"Tony, I need to know if you've seen Everly."

I glanced at the television. They were back to an interview with Everly. She was there in front of me, in full Technicolor, flanked on either side by ugly flower arrangements, and with a large black-and-white picture of Hope cradled in her arms. She was talking about Hope, promising the world that Hope would *never* up and disappear. My stomach roiled, anger like a tight fist sitting in my gut.

"Tony?"

"Uh…I saw her at the vigil."

"But after that? Did you see her after that?"

"I left the vigil early."

The camera panned to the brokenhearted Jensens, then floated back to Everly, who nodded her head emphatically, her blond curls a golden halo around her head. I reached out and muted the volume, unwilling to hear Everly pledge her support for her missing *friend*.

"Can you tell me what this is about?"

Mrs. Byer sucked in a short, loud breath. "I'm calling everyone on her contacts list."

"Okay." I pressed the television's power button and the set flashed off, leaving Everly in midsentence, her wide eyes huge. Her outline stained my television monitor; her image hovered, ghost-like, for a moment before fading to black.

"Everly didn't come home last night."

THIRTY-NINE

Hope

When my eyes flew open, I felt safe. My blankets cradled me, and the lavender-silver paint was soft on my eyes…until I moved. Until I lost that murky cloud of sleep. Then the sheets were stiff and new, unwashed. The paint still smelled fresh. The pillows had jagged, just-out-of-the-package edges, and the stuffed animal that Daniel had placed beside me—a brand-new replica of the shaggy bear I'd had since birth—sat and stared down at me, his limbs still plump with factory-new cotton, the thread used to make his lips a deep bloodred. The color had faded to a chic pink on my bear at home.

Home.

The tears started before I registered an emotion.

I kicked off the covers and sat bolt-upright. And who really knew? Maybe it was. Suddenly, my skin felt like it was on fire or shrouded in filth. I wanted a shower. I wanted to be clean, to have Daniel and this moment and this horrible fake slice of my life bleached out of my skin, purged from my body.

I ripped the stuffed animals from the shelves, then yanked at the shelves, willing them to move. They didn't. I took *my* lamp by its weak neck and slammed it hard against the wall, waiting for the sweet release of shattering plaster, but the thing just bounced off the wall with a useless thunk. I tossed it. I tore at the carpet and used my fingernails to rake at the paint.

There were bloody streaks on the wall, streaks of tears down my face. I was locked in here, in this place I should have known. I was going to die. I was going to die, or Daniel was going to kill me. The reality was overwhelming and sickening. My knees buckled, and I sat hard on the carpet, curled into myself, and cried.

Why was this happening?

"I've been watching you…"

The tears came faster then, huge, body-racking sobs that made my throat parched and my head throb.

How did Daniel know me?

I called up his image in my mind, even as it made my stomach ache.

Daniel. Did I know him?

How?

I bit into my lip as I examined every inch of him from memory: Those eyes. Set too wide, sleepy, milky almost. The lazy slope of his nose, bulbous at the end. Lips that curved into those hideous, stomach-churning grins.

Did I know him?

"Hope?" Daniel was at the door, his voice muffled. He didn't wait for me to answer as the locks began to slip. With each one,

I shrank into myself, trying to make myself smaller, to disappear into the dingy mattress, these sheets that were my sheets but weren't. Then Daniel was standing in the doorway, and I kicked back my covers and sat bolt upright, unwilling to give him any ideas. I pressed my feet into the carpet, felt every muscle in my body tighten. I tried to inch away, to scoot to the bottom half of the bed, but I could only make it past the midway point before the clamp around my ankle tightened, before the cold metal dug against my bone, recut into the already puckered and broken skin there.

"I thought we'd go for a picnic today," he said with a grin, like we were some kind of blissful couple.

"I'm not going on a picnic with you. I'm not going anywhere with you."

He completely ignored me, stepped back into the hall, and wheeled a little two-shelved cart into my room. On the second shelf was a tray of gray-looking food: a mound of something that might have been scrambled eggs, two pieces of toast cut on the diagonal, two lines of fat-bubbled bacon, and a mug of oil-slick coffee. My stomach lurched. On the top shelf was an ancient-looking TV with knobs, fat buttons, and a pair of antennae that look like rabbit ears.

"Well." Daniel took my breakfast tray and set it on the desk, then plugged the TV into the outlet. "We were going to go for a picnic for lunch today, but it's a little drizzly. A much better day to stay home anyway. And besides, your buddies have arranged a little search party for you."

The picture on the TV wobbled and faded. Daniel manipulated the rabbit ears, and the picture cleared up a tiny bit. It was still fuzzy, still gray, but I lost my breath when I saw the school come into focus, the card table with Ashleigh and Renee behind it, and—yes, that was him!—Tony standing in the background. The television reporter was interviewing one of the campus cops who looked like a kid playing a role. He had his arms crossed in front of his chest, legs askew, but even in that tough-guy stance, he looked like he was wearing a Halloween costume.

"Bruce and Becky Jensen are teaming up with the police department, the campus community police"—here the officer flashed a toothy grin—"and *Wake Up the Bay!* to do a grid search of August Woods in an attempt to find Hope or any evidence that might lead us to her. Volunteers or those interested in participating can come here to the school to sign up or check in with the police department prior to meeting tonight at the J Parking Lot off Flynn Street."

I saw Daniel stiffen, and hope flared up in my gut. If he didn't want to take me out while they were searching, maybe it was because they were close and they would find me… But Daniel flapped a hand at the wobbly picture on screen and smiled at me like I was in on the joke.

"It's nice that they're all coming out to help you, huh? Too bad they're searching in the wrong place. Now…" He turned, took the tray of grayish food, and plopped it on my bed. "You need to eat, Hope. You need to keep your strength up. It's not going to do either of us much good if you get sick, now is it?"

I reached for the tray, ready to fling it, but Daniel grabbed my arm and held me with a stare that was ice cold. "Eat it."

"I'm not going to."

He sat on the edge of the bed, just the weight of him causing my mattress to groan and throwing up pinprick warning signs all over my body. *Don't let him get too close… Don't let him get near me…* He pulled a plastic fork from a sealed cellophane bag and handed it to me. "See? You can trust me. Perfectly safe."

"What about the food? How do I know you're not trying to poison me?"

His face fell. "Poison you? Why would I do that? Hope…" He inched toward me, and I watched the black coffee slosh from the cup and soak the edge of the toast. "Why would I try to hurt you? I love you."

The admission made my skin crawl, made every inch of my skin tighten, made my muscles seize up. "But you are hurting me." I held up my leg and gave him a good view of the gouge around my ankle. "If you really loved me…"

"I do." Daniel pumped his head. "That's from you. That"—he jabbed a finger toward my leg—"is only because you don't love me yet." He smiled, the look terribly confident and serene. "You will. Now"—he dug the fork into the eggs and brought them to my mouth—"eat."

"No."

He softly pressed the fork tines against my lower lip. "Eat, Hope."

I opened my mouth and let a miniscule bite of food cross my

lips. I chewed obediently just to make Daniel happy, hoping then he would leave me alone.

It worked.

"See? Isn't that better?"

I forced the food down and offered a tight-lipped half smile. "I'm done now."

Daniel frowned, blew out a sigh, then tossed his hands up in the air. "I'm doing the best I can for you, Hope."

I gritted my teeth, feeling the pasty eggs trying to come back up. He clapped his hands, the sound making me jump. Then he laughed.

"You're jumpy!"

I didn't answer.

"Well, you'll get more comfortable soon. You can watch TV for a bit, okay?"

I nodded as the television flickered, casting a weird strobe-light effect through my room. Even though the walls were painted my favorite color and the stuffed animals and posters made the room light, there was a darkness here that was palpable.

"I'm going to be gone for awhile, okay?" Daniel reached into his pocket and pulled out a handful of granola bars in wrinkled wrappers. The bars were misshapen and looked like they had been in his pocket forever. He laid the bars on my desk, arranging them one by one is a straight line, lining up the edges just so.

"I have to check in to work, but I'll be back later, and then we'll have a nice dinner. Okay? Would you like that, Hope?"

I sat stolid, unmoving. There was nothing left in me.

"Hope?"

He leaned down, his face a half inch from mine. Snapped his fingers right in front of my nose.

"Sure." I pushed the word out.

"That's a good girl."

FORTY

Tony

Everly didn't come home.

Mrs. Byer had said that she was missing. She had used that exact word before she hung up: "Tony, Everly has gone missing." She didn't accuse me, didn't insinuate, but I knew that she would. And soon everyone else would too. My heart started slamming against my rib cage. My pulse ratcheted up.

Mrs. Byer had called me from Everly's phone, the phone she left behind.

Hope had left behind her phone too.

Maybe Everly was faking it too.

Pulling a Hope.

I stood there in my bedroom shaking.

FORTY-ONE

Hope

I watched Daniel walk away, watched him carefully pull the door shut behind him and slide the locks: one, two, three. Each click was like another nail in my coffin. One: my last breaths. Two: dying. Three: dead.

I heard his footsteps plod down the hall, heard him click off the TV in the front room. Silence again, until the front door slammed and Daniel cranked the engine of his car.

He left me alone in this room that I should know, this room that was a sad replica of a life that I thought I knew. I turned back to the ancient television on the ratty cart and focused hard on the faded screen. My parents, perched on the edges of their morning show set chairs, the fake ficus in between them. My mother laughed, the sound a high, light tinkling I had never appreciated. My father patted her on the thigh. They shared a look, unspoken words, a conversation I had never been privy to.

Their television world went on, while mine crashed and burned.

FORTY-TWO

Tony

The homage to Hope took over one entire wall of the gym. It had grown from posters and flowers to teddy bears and candles that stayed lit. Balloons bobbed in the wind. Cellophane flower wrappers crackled, and glitter was all over the place.

We love you, Hope.

We'll find you, Hope.

We'll never stop looking for you, Hope.

Posters. Fliers. Banners. Everyone talked in hushed, respectful tones. Hope's name on everyone's lips. Teachers had pictures of her in their rooms; the principal made daily announcements. Grief counselors. Police officers. "If you know anything, anything at all, please contact Officer Pace or Officer MacNamara…"

FORTY-THREE

Hope

After I was unchained, I rubbed my fingertips raw going over the walls, pressing into every corner looking for a weak spot or a seam. I pulled at the carpet, rooted through the closet. I tried to yank the curtain rods down, worked out how I could strangle Daniel with the gauzy drapes.

In the first few hours, I had plans.

But as daylight started to wane, so did I.

I was lying on the bed rereading one of the books Daniel had left me, when I heard the engine roar, heard the *ping-ping-ping* of gravel on steel. I stood on my tiptoes, pressed my nose against the just-barely-too-high window, and watched Daniel's truck pull up the drive. He killed the engine, and I studied him as he got out of the car. Stocky build, baseball cap pulled low over his eyes.

Did I know him?

Thick neck, burst of dark hair brushing the pale-blue collar of his shirt.

Think, Hope! Did I recognize him?

Bulbous nose, thin lips constantly pulled into that gargoyle grimace.

I shot through my mental contacts list and tried to call up everyone I had ever met as Daniel came closer. He was carrying a grocery bag close to his chest, and I studied that too, desperate for any clue, any indication as to where I was or what was nearby besides the endless trees and useless stretch of highway that I already knew.

I came up with nothing. I didn't recognize Daniel. I didn't recognize the name, Bi-Rite, on the grocery bag. My throat constricted, and tears flooded my eyes. I would never get out of here. No one would ever find me.

And then I noticed the patch stitched to the shoulder of his pale blue button-down.

Atlas Security.

The patch was red and white, and I'd seen it a thousand times. Atlas Security patrolled the neighborhood at home. Patrolled the lot where *Wake Up the Bay!* was shot. There was a handful of different guards, most as benign and nondescript-looking at Daniel.

I watched as he straightened his shirt. Then, to my relief, he removed the huge flashlight he had hanging from a belt loop and tossed it back in the car. He took off a cheap-looking walkie-talkie as well, and when he turned, I studied every inch of him, looking for weapons. I was pretty sure that security guards didn't carry guns—but I knew that Daniel had one.

If it wasn't on him, where was it?

I watched Daniel like he was my prey. He shifted the grocery bag from one arm to the other. He came walking toward me.

From my room, I could hear him jam the key in the door, could hear the locks as they tumbled.

"I'm home!" he called. His happy, singsong voice exploded ice water through my veins, and I was panting, breathing hard, hate mixed with anger and fear enveloping me fully.

"Hope, are you awake?"

My heart thundered in my throat, choking me. I prayed to die. Let a heart attack kill me before Daniel could lay a finger on me.

"Hope?" He pulled the door open and stood there, grinning. "How are you?"

"You work at the security company. At Atlas."

This seemed to make Daniel beam. "You do remember me?"

I didn't answer, and he took a step toward me, reaching out a hand. I willed my legs to move, to propel me backward to hide or forward to pounce, but I was once again a thousand useless pounds, an immovable mass of wet cement as Daniel approached.

"We had something special. I knew you felt it. You just had to remember it."

I blinked and pressed my teeth into my bottom lip to stop myself from crying.

"I've watched you since the very beginning."

It was then that I heard the voices again. Low, wafting from the television screen: my parents. Bruce and Becky Jensen, images of perfection. Mom, Dad, and me, the perfect family.

"Please…" It was my mother, her voice cracked and choked with sorrow. "Please, if you know anything, if you have any information about our daughter, Hope, contact the number on your screen. No questions asked. We just want our daughter back."

And then another voice. Younger. Honey-sweet.

"Hope is my best friend. I know that she would come back to us if she could. Please, please, if you have Hope, just let her go…"

I knew that voice. Everly Byer.

They were looking. Everyone was out looking for me.

I would be saved.

Daniel shook his head slowly as if reading my thoughts, and anxiety pinballed through me.

No.

"They're looking for me," I said, pushing the words over cracked, dry lips. "They're going to find me."

Tears welled up and fell over my cheeks, and I let them, my whole body trembling. I could still hear Everly, could hear the newscaster breaking in and asking her questions. There had been a vigil. There were search parties and helicopters, and I would be saved. I looked around at the horrible lavender walls, at yet another attempt to falsify my life, and the ridiculous humor of it bubbled up inside me, and *I laughed.*

"I'm going to get out of here. You're not going to be able to keep me here because they're going to find you. They're going to find me."

The smile dropped from Daniel's lips. "No, Hope. You can't count on them. And…" He shrugged and looked around. "No one's going to find you here."

The television voices continued to waft into the room. *"We'll never stop looking for you, Hope."*

"They don't really care," Daniel said. He cocked his head, listening for a beat. "Sure, it sounds like they do. They put on a really good show." He nodded emphatically, and I could see the white spot on his scalp where I'd tugged out his hair. It should have made me happy, but I was intent, listening to the voices on the television screen.

My mother: *"Please just bring our daughter back."*

"I was there last night, Hope. I was there."

My father: *"Any information you have. No questions asked."*

"It wasn't about you. It has never been about you."

"Please. We need our daughter back."

"This…" Daniel spread out his hands, gestured to me, to himself, to the room. "This is about you. I'm all about you. They aren't. They are all about themselves, Hope. Don't you see? They're all phonies. You know that. She's not true. Your best friend, Everly? She's not being true."

The hope started to leave my body, but I gritted my teeth and balled my fists.

"They *will* find me."

Again, Daniel shook his head, that weird, sad smile on his lips. "It's too late for that, Hope."

FORTY-FOUR

Tony

Alice was watching *Paw Patrol* with my mother when I came into the living room.

"Where's Dad?" I asked.

My mother didn't answer me, just jutted her chin toward the garage. "Can I make you some breakfast?" She didn't look at me and eyed the clock instead. "Or lunch?"

"No, thanks. But can I turn on the news?"

I went for the remote control, but my mother stopped me with one hand on the remote, the other on Alice's arm. "Alice is watching this."

Mom pinned me with a gaze. Then I knew that she knew. The news about Everly going missing must be out too.

I dialed Bellingham.

"Don't talk to anyone."

"Hello?" I said.

"Tony, don't talk to anyone. The press, the police."

"About?"

"You haven't heard about Everly?"

Deflation. "Her mother called me."

"Look, there is no official word, and as of now, it's not even an investigation. It hasn't even been twelve hours."

I nodded, though Bellingham couldn't see me.

"Just don't talk to anyone."

I glanced back at Alice, at my mother who turned the volume up. I cupped my hand over the phone and went to the kitchen, then sat in the same spot where Everly had sat that night she came over. "If it's not even news yet, how come everyone seems to know? How come you know?"

"I'm your attorney. I know everything. You can thank me later."

Bellingham's attempt at lightness fell flat.

"I have a police scanner and a friend at 911 dispatch. And a friend on the police force."

"You have a lot of friends." I knew it sounded stupid, but it was the only thing I could think of to say.

Bellingham didn't respond.

"Mr. Bellingham? Mr. Bellingham?"

I could hear crackling and chatting on his end of the phone. Then, "Oh my God."

"Mr. Bellingham? Is something going? Mr.—"

Another crackle, another sputter, and I realized that Bellingham was listening to his police scanner.

"Sit tight right there, Tony, and don't talk to anyone. Not anyone at all."

"Wait, what?"

"The police have just recovered a body."

"A-a body?" I stuttered.

"Female. Young adult. Slight frame. Blond."

My stomach went to liquid.

* * *

I sat in my house and stared at the phone for hours, willing it to ring.

It didn't.

I sat at the dining room table, my eyes intent on the front door. I figured Pace and MacNamara would knock at any minute, would be waiting to haul me away. When the knock finally did come, I was rooted to the chair. I couldn't move. Then Bellingham let himself in. We stared at each other for a silent beat. Wordlessly, I implored him to tell me that it wasn't Hope, that this wasn't happening, that everything was going to be okay. He let out a long sigh and raked a hand through his hair.

"Is it her?"

"The police haven't released a statement yet."

"Is. It. Her?" My words were slow and even. I needed Bellingham to tell me something.

"The police—"

"Screw the police. What do your friends say? You have friends everywhere, right? Don't they know?"

Bellingham put a hand on my shoulder and pushed me down so that I was sitting. "I don't know anything yet, Tony. But I can assure you, the moment I do, I'll let you know. Now, is there anything you need to tell me? Anything—" He paused and took a deep, slow breath, his gaze pinning mine, "—you think I should know?"

The saliva soured in my mouth. The whole room fish-eyed, then snapped back to proportion.

"You think I hurt her." I was incredulous.

Bellingham went palms forward. "All I asked was if there was anything you wanted to say to me. Anything you wanted to talk to me about."

I couldn't look at Bellingham. "Like a confession."

He didn't answer.

"I didn't do this," I said slowly. "I didn't…"

Bellingham gathered his jacket and looked like he was going to say something before thinking better of it. He crossed the living room and paused, his hand on the doorknob. "I just need you to sit tight here, okay, Tony? Just sit tight until you hear from me."

I sat at the dining room table until Alice went back to her bedroom with her *Frozen* mug to take a nap. Until an unrecognized number flashed on my cell phone screen.

"Hello?"

"Hey, Tony." Long pause. Throat clearing. "It's Rustin."

I pulled the phone from my ear, looked at the number on the readout, then pushed the phone back. "Rustin? What do you want?"

Another long pause. Then, "I need to talk to you about Hope."

FORTY-FIVE

Tony

Rustin wanted me to meet him in the parking lot of an abandoned grocery store. I took the same exit where I had followed him on the day we fought, the same exit I took on the night of the vigil. He gave me directions based on landmarks rather than street names: go left at the old ski chalet, hang a right at that circle of pine trees. I did four switchbacks and considered turning around before a cracked road deposited me in the grocery store parking lot.

Rustin was already there. He was sitting in his car when I pulled up. I parked next to him, but he didn't seem to notice me. I rolled down my window and killed the engine.

"Hey," I said.

He blinked a couple of times but didn't acknowledge me, and something dark settled in my gut as fear crept from the base of my spine. My head whipped around the empty lot, suddenly certain that this was some kind of trap, that Rustin's goons would start popping out of oblivion with baseball bats and chains, ready to pulverize me. Nothing happened.

"Rustin?"

He gripped the steering wheel, licked his lips, then finally turned to look at me. I could see that his eyes were glossy, red-rimmed, like he'd been crying.

"I don't know where she is," he said finally.

I got out of my car and crouched so I was staring into his window. "What?"

"Hope." He blinked. "I don't know where Hope is."

I nodded slowly. "Okay."

He blew out a defeated sigh. "You were right. She planned the whole thing, and I went along with it." Rustin's eyes raked over me, something like hatred in them. "She just wanted to teach you a lesson, and I figured what the hell? It was all in good fun."

I bit back bile. *All in good fun*, and I was on my way to jail.

"I took Hope to my parents' cabin in the woods. She was just supposed to stay there a day or two." He shrugged. "No big deal."

"So you were buying her food."

"Yeah." He gestured to the floorboard on the passenger side. A grocery bag sat there, a can of Pringles sticking out, nestled between some hummus and another package of mini muffins. "I was going to bring her this last stash and be done with it. I was over the whole thing, and it got blown way out of proportion. The stuff on the news, the candlelight vigil."

"And?"

"And I went to the cabin, but Hope wasn't there."

I crossed my arms in front of my chest. "So?"

"So she was supposed to be there. She had no way of leaving. No car."

"She probably just went for a walk or something." I shrugged, anger burning in the pit of my stomach. Rustin had helped Hope pull one over on me. And now he was sad because Hope had left him? I would have laughed. I should have. That was Hope. Your best friend one minute, a royal bitch the next.

"So what are you telling me this for? What do you want from me?"

Rustin shook his head. "I figured maybe she went for a walk or something last night. But she wasn't back this morning." Rustin looked at me, and now I could see there was actual fear in his eyes. "And she wasn't now either."

Bellingham's words came back to me: *The police have just recovered a body.*

"Take me to where you took her."

Rustin screwed up his face. "What?"

"Take me to where you stashed Hope."

"She's not there. I told you."

I glared, and Rustin blew out a low sigh, but he gestured for me to get in the car. I did, and he turned the key in the ignition. We were silent as he threw his car in gear and slowly pulled out of the parking lot.

My mind whirred as the forest around us got denser, doubt hanging at the edge of my periphery. What if this was just another part of Hope's plan? What if Everly was in on it, and they were all just trying to teach me a lesson? I shifted in my seat, and Rustin looked at me, a muscle in his jaw flicking.

"You okay, bro?"

"Tell me about Hope's plan."

Rustin frowned, not taking his eyes off the tree-lined stretch of highway in front of us. "What?"

I raised my eyebrows, and he nodded. "It wasn't all that super-detailed or anything. I was there when Hope called you that night."

I swallowed, the lump in my throat rising fast. *That night…*

"We were just screwing around. Hope was only going to be gone a day or two. She dumped her cell phone, forwarded most everything to a new one and"—Rustin shrugged—"that was pretty much it."

"She didn't say anything to her parents?"

Rustin snorted. "You know her parents. We were both surprised that they even noticed she was gone."

I nodded. "And then what?"

"Then nothing. It wasn't supposed to be a big thing… At least I didn't think it was supposed to be. She was going to be gone for, like, a day or two. You'd feel super bad, she'd come back to school, and that would be that."

Anger boiled inside me. *That would be that.* I had a lawyer. I had been interrogated by the police. My parents couldn't even look at me.

That would be that.

That was Hope. Nothing mattered but getting her revenge.

And now she was missing.

229

Was she?

"And what about Everly?"

Rustin took an easy corner, letting his foot off the gas. "What about her?"

"What was her role?"

"Nothing. Like I said, no big fancy plan. Just what I told you. Except…" His voice trailed off as he squinted down the dark road.

"Except?"

"The thing got out of hand. Her parents got involved. The police. The whole vigil and all the specials. I wanted to tell Hope I was done. I could get in real trouble for that shit, you know?"

I knew.

"So I texted her, but she didn't answer. Called her. No answer. Finally, I went up to the house and"—another shrug—"she wasn't there."

Rustin took a blink-and-you'd-miss-it turnoff and slowed to a crawl. I could hear the pebbles from the dirt road plinking off the car, could feel the crunch of gravel underneath as we pulled down a narrow drive, a plain clapboard house framed by redwoods coming into view.

"She was supposed to be here," Rustin said, his voice choked.

He parked the car, and I followed him, keeping a good pace behind, my ears pricked for anything that could be a warning: Hope's giggle as she watched from somewhere. Everly's whisper as they waited for me. But there was nothing. At the porch, I hung back.

"Dude," Rustin said over his shoulder, "you coming?"

I nodded, waited for him to push open the door and step inside before I joined him. The place was decent but a mess: a small living room with mismatched furniture pushed askew. A broken leg on the table, but a nicer TV than the one we had at home. A stash of grocery bags on the kitchen counter. An empty bag of baby carrots was in the garbage can; the package of mini muffins on the coffee table.

Nice enough place, but not exactly Hope's style.

"So I'm just supposed to believe that Hope has been hanging out here for a week?"

But Rustin didn't answer me. I turned to see that he was picking something up off the porch. Hope's hoodie.

My stomach clenched.

Still, I told myself, *that doesn't mean anything.*

"This is Hope's."

Rustin looked at the discarded hoodie. His face had gone ash white, his mouth hanging open. He shook his head slowly. "I didn't do this, man. I didn't tie her up. I dropped her off. She was fine. I got her the blueberry mini muffins." He looked like the mini muffin run was a holy baptism. I wanted to rip his head off.

"What part of the plan is this, Rustin? Is this part of it? You lead me up here, and she's supposedly"—I slapped at the hoodie—"been hauled off by some madman or something? You're as fucked up as she is." I stomped out of the room, sure if I stayed another moment I'd have Rustin by the throat up against one of those lame-ass, plaid-flannel paintings that were all over the walls. Rustin ran up behind me.

"Man, I'm serious. There wasn't anything else. I was supposed to pick her up, and she was just supposed to...you know, be here."

"Then where the hell is she?"

Rustin started to tremble, his eyes taking up his full face. "I don't know."

I should have cared about Rustin, but I was too freaked out, too pissed. I grabbed him by the shirt and thumped him against the wall. "Who else knows about this place?"

"Here? No one. I mean, my mom and dad and..." Rustin wouldn't meet my eye. I shook him again.

"Who else?"

"I don't know. I don't know how anyone would know that she was out here."

I let Rustin down and raked a hand through my hair, looking around the small place. "Is there any way she could have gone somewhere on her own?"

"I don't know, man. I guess if someone else was in on..."

"You don't know?"

"I thought I did. But you know Hope."

I didn't.

"Call her," I said.

"Huh?"

"You said she had a new phone. Call her. See if she answers."

"I've been—"

"Call. Her."

Rustin finally nodded and obediently pulled out his phone.

"Put it on speaker."

He dialed, flipped the phone on speaker, and we both waited for the connection.

"It's ringing."

I cocked my head, my eyes going wide. "It's ringing here."

The sound was low, muffled, but unmistakable. Hope's phone was inside the house.

I started yanking pillows off the couch.

Rustin held his phone out but jumped in, shaking out an afghan and rifling through a stack of magazines.

"Where is it?"

I dropped to my knees, peering under the couch. It was still plugged in and must have fallen. "Here!"

"She left her phone. She would never leave her phone."

"She did once before."

Rustin nodded. "Yeah. Yeah." He pumped his head. "Maybe she's just messing with me too, you know? Maybe…" He blew out an unconvincing half snort, half laugh. "Maybe she's just messing with me too."

"We have to go to the police, man. Or at least her parents."

Rustin paled and paused for a beat. "No, not right now. I mean, she's Hope, right? She's probably…"

"Everly didn't come home last night," I said slowly.

"Well, there you have it. Everly probably came by and picked up Hope. The two are probably halfway to Mexico right now. You know? Probably laughing their asses off at us."

Part of me wanted to believe him. Part of me wanted to be like him and believe again that Hope was playing a prank, that everything would blow over with Hope staging a big *Ta-da!* at the end. But there was a body in the woods.

"We're going to the police," I said.

"No, no way."

"Hope could be in trouble."

Rustin seemed to consider that, seemed to savor the idea a bit. Then he shook his head again. "No, she's not."

"If you didn't believe Hope was in trouble, you wouldn't have called me."

He dug his hands in his back pockets, suddenly the picture of cool. "Yeah, well, I'm beginning to see that was a mistake."

"Whatever, dude. Let's just go." I turned and pulled the door open. "You coming, or do you want me to drive?"

"We're not going to the police, okay? Hope is probably fine. She and—"

"She and Everly took off. Some grand prank. I get it. We're going to go tell the police and let them handle it." I left the house, didn't check to see if Rustin was following me. And then I stopped.

I could see them clearly now: tire tracks. Thick and heavy in the mud. But the tracks weren't what made my stomach drop, made me catch my breath. It was the tracks that stopped where the tire tread started. Footprints. First two pairs, one small and erratic. Then a single pair. I could see where someone had dug their feet in. Where they tried to hold their ground. And I could see where that person had been dragged away.

FORTY-SIX

Hope

Thoughts ricocheted through my head at a mile a minute. "Too late for what? Daniel?"

But he didn't answer me. Then, "We're going to be so happy together." Another one of those weird, gargoyle smiles that made my blood run cold. "No one is coming for you, Hope."

I shook my head. "My parents…" My voice was a raspy whisper. "My parents will find me."

"Your parents." Daniel chuckled. "They're getting so famous."

"You know them."

"How do you think I found you?"

I sat there, stunned, paralyzed, as Daniel stood up, crossed the room, then silently shut the door behind him.

Daniel had found me at a remote cabin in the woods. My parents. *They're getting so famous… How do you think I found you?*

No.

They wouldn't.

How far would they go for fame?

The locks slid: one, two, three. Nails in my coffin.

FORTY-SEVEN

Tony

I kept Rustin's black car in my rearview mirror as we left the old grocery store, wound down the highway, and came back into town. Halfway there, the traffic crawled to a standstill, and I pounded the steering wheel.

My thoughts were fragmented and fast. I was seething mad that Hope had plotted this revenge but not wholly surprised. I wondered whether her parents were in on it, whether the entire Channel 7 news team was in on it—and then I remembered: *They found a body.*

I shifted in my seat and plucked at my shirt, which was stuck to me with a sheen of sweat. It couldn't have been Hope…

Then Ava Byer's words came back to me: *Everly didn't come home last night.*

I should have expected that the police would come to me.

Pace was at the side of the road with four other uniformed officers. There was a line of police cars, lights flashing, the reason for the achingly slow crawl of traffic. The police had cordoned off the entrance to August Woods. The coroner's van was parked out front, and news crews and reporters were clamoring for footing behind metal police barricades. The line of cars on the road all slowed, drivers and passengers rubbernecking, heads craning to see what was going on.

In my rearview mirror, I could see Rustin, see the color rising in his cheeks as Pace approached my car and leaned in my open window.

"How are you doing, Tony?" He sounded genuinely curious.

"Actually, I want to talk to you…to the police."

Pace seemed taken aback. "I think that's a really wise decision."

"I have some information. And"—I swallowed hard—"I think Hope might really be in trouble."

Pace looked over his shoulder at the crowd assembled. "I know she is."

FORTY-EIGHT

Hope

I couldn't focus on my parents. I refused to believe that they had something to do with this, with Daniel, with anything. I was their prop, their ticket to better ratings, but…

Had they known?

My throat was parched, and being in this room had sucked every bit of moisture from my body. I didn't want to ask Daniel for anything. I didn't want him to think I depended on him, *needed* him, but I realized with soul-splitting pain that I *did*.

I knocked gently first, a soft, dainty set of three little raps.

"Daniel?" Thirst choked my voice, made it raspy and weak. I knocked harder when there was no response. "Daniel?"

I waited, pressing my ear against the door, trying to discern my heartbeat from Daniel's footsteps. I both desperately wanted him to answer, to unlock the door, and to be gone, far away from me, from this place.

There was no response from the other side of the door.

I slammed my fists against the heavy wood. "*Daniel!* Someone! Anyone! *Help!*"

I didn't know how long I kept up the tirade, but the sky outside the long, high window went from misty black to inky, and the skin on the edges of my hands was purpled and puckered and cracked. I fell to my knees, then my butt, and crumbled against the door frame, waiting, begging, feeling more and more pitiful.

And then I heard it.

An engine roaring. A door slamming. Footsteps clattering down the hall.

I used every last inch of strength I had to push myself up. "Daniel?" I thumbed the door, leaving bloody imprints. "Daniel?" My voice sounded weak and rough.

The locks slid.

One, two, three.

Then, "Get away from the door, Hope."

I fumbled, took two steps backward.

Daniel appeared in the doorway, shimmied in, and sank a key into the lock behind him. I realized with a painful start that the click was the sound of a lock sliding.

I didn't know what was worse: Daniel being locked on the outside or here with me on the inside.

He looked disheveled and sweaty, his hair mussed, the collar of his shirt torn. There was a long, red scratch down his left cheek, and he seemed to be breathing hard.

"Are you hungry?"

I wanted to ask him where he'd been. I wanted to know where

he went, what happened on the other side of this locked door, but I didn't dare. All I could do was nod, my eyes glued to the McDonald's bag he held in one fist, glued to the beads of condensation that stood out on the large cup he was holding.

He held both out to me, and I snatched them hungrily, then crawled back to a corner of my room, sinking down to the floor, keeping one wild eye on him while my lips closed around the straw.

I should have wondered whether he poisoned the drink. I should have been concerned the cheeseburger was drug laced. But I was starving. Everything was cold, but I didn't care. I shoveled it in, even though my stomach ached.

Daniel smiled. "It's good to see you eat. Sorry it's so late tonight. It won't always be like this." He looked at his hands, and I could see that they were filthy, dirt-caked, worse than usual. He wiped his palms on his jeans. "I had something I had to take care of." He turned, then paused and fished an apple pie out of his back pocket. He held it out to me. "I got you this too. Here."

I chewed, but didn't move.

"Go on."

I pulled a single fry out of my bag.

He shrugged and put the apple pie on the edge of the desk. His shirtsleeve rode up as he did, and I could see the scratches all over his forearm, blooming red and green at the jagged edges. I stared until he turned and unlocked the door, took the key, and slid it down the lanyard around his neck.

"Sleep tight, Hope. Everything's all better now."

FORTY-NINE

Tony

For once, every newscast wasn't about Hope. Her pictures didn't dominate the newspaper. There was just a tiny shot of her in the upper left-hand corner on the front page, not even in color. Another girl took her place. Another blond with her head thrown back, perfect white teeth showing in her toothy grin: Everly Byer.

My parents tried to hide the paper. It was the recycling can before I even got up, but Alice went after it, drawing stick figures and lopsided flowers around the giant black headline: Body of Teen Girl Found in August Woods Identified.

> A resident walking her dog alerted authorities to a body found in a shallow grave about fifteen feet off the running trail at August Woods last night. Police initially confirmed the body was of a teenage girl, approximately fifteen to eighteen years of age, but identification wasn't released until just before press time. Authorities initially feared

the body might belong to Florence resident Hope Jensen, seventeen, but the identification of Everly Byer did little to quell residents' anguish and fears.

"First the Jensen girl goes missing, then another turns up dead? What's going on?" Shayla Murphy, who regularly uses the August Woods running trail, spoke to the *Herald*. "I never felt unsafe in this community until now. These two beautiful girls… Someone is out to get them. Someone is out to get all of us."

I threw the paper in the trash and turned on the compactor. It had barely started to smash everything down when my phone rang.

"Hello?"

"Tony, it's me." Bellingham. "I assume you've seen the papers, seen the news?"

I opened my mouth to answer, but Bellingham rushed on. "This is a disaster."

I thought of Everly at my house, the way she smelled when she whirled, the same jasmine-scented cloud that followed Hope. I thought of her lips pressed against mine, the earnestness in her eyes…the way she disappeared silently out my door.

"I can't believe she's…" I didn't want to say the word. I couldn't bring myself to say the word because if I did, it would be true. All of this would be true.

"I need to know where you were last night. The last two nights."

"Here. I have barely left the house. But what does it matter where I was?" The weight of knowing walloped me, and I physically lost my balance and had to sit down. "They're not going to think I had anything to do with—"

"They already do. The media and the police have already put together that it was Everly who left your house the other night. Now you're connected to two missing young women. It's not looking good for you, Tony."

I could feel all the blood run out of my face. It felt like it was rushing out of my body. I felt like I should have been gagging, vomiting, passing out, crying, but nothing happened. I just sat there, stunned, numb.

"I didn't have anything to—"

"I know, kid. I've heard the speech. You didn't have anything to do with either of them. You can tell me till you're blue in the face. You're going to have to tell the media and the cops until you *are* blue in the face, but they've got to believe you. I need to know your every step. I need to know if there is something you're not telling me, something you're trying to hide. I don't care if you did it or not."

Finally, it was like I woke up. "If I did it? Do you really think I could have done this? Killed Everly, done something to Hope? Because maybe you shouldn't be defending me if you don't believe that I would never, ever do something like that. I mean..." I sprang up and started to pace. "If you think I'm guilty, shouldn't I find a different attorney?"

"The law isn't about guilt or innocence."

I gaped. "Yes it is!"

"I appreciate your naïveté, and most people don't have to learn this lesson until much later in life. You're going to be tried and likely convicted before we ever set foot in the courtroom. Turn on the TV. It's happening right now."

I went for the remote control. Switched channels frantically, with the volume off. Three channels back to back. Three talking heads. My picture was in the corner on Channel 7. Shots of Everly and Hope on a split screen while a news ticker ran underneath on Channel 5. A law professor from Florence State University on Channel 2, the headline plastered across his neat gray suit asking *Is He Guilty?*

My heart slammed against my chest.

I couldn't catch a full breath.

"Sit down, Tony, sit down. Head between your knees. Can you breathe? It sounds like you're hyperventilating. You okay? Head between your knees, breathe slowly and deeply."

I didn't know why, but I was listening to everything Bellingham said. I pulled out a dining room chair, sat down hard, and dropped my head between my knees. Tried to breathe.

"Deep breath in, slow breath out."

My lungs felt like they were in my throat, like they were going to drop out of my mouth.

Finally I asked, "People really think I'm capable of this?"

"It's the media, Tony. It's the cops. High-pressure case… The cops are under a lot of stress from the Jensens and the community to solve this crime."

"*I* want them to solve this crime."

Mr. Bellingham's voice went soft. "I know, kid. But solving the crime doesn't always mean they've got the right guy. Right now, they're under pressure to solve the crime fast, to open and shut the case regardless."

"But they're going after the wrong guy! If they lock me up, then people are still going to die! Hope is…is…still…"

I could feel the breath start to leave me again.

"Deep breaths, Tony."

"I want to talk to them. I want to tell my side. I want to tell them I'm not guilty! I have to."

Long pause. I could hear Bellingham sucking his teeth. "I'm not so sure that's a great idea."

I was up again, pacing. "I can tell them I didn't do this. I dated Hope and we broke up and it was hard on me, but I didn't hurt her… I didn't—"

Share Location?

That goddamn curser flashed in my mind again.

Everly's lips brushed over mine again.

She slipped out the back door and into the black, black night.

Everly died.

"I didn't do this…"

The phone went dead. Hope went missing.

Share Location?

I had to come clean. I had to tell everything I knew. It was too late for Everly, but it might not be too late for Hope…right?

Share Location?

"I want to go on TV," I told Bellingham. "I don't care what you say. I want to go on TV and tell them. It might be the only way to save Hope."

"Or it could be the final nail in your coffin, Tony."

I gritted my teeth and fisted my hands so hard my nails dug into my flesh. The blood that bubbled up was itchy, sticky, but I kept pushing.

"I want to talk to the media."

FIFTY

Hope

I could hear Daniel on the other side of the door. He was in the kitchen, shuffling pots and pans. I listened, ear pressed against the cold wood until I heard the footsteps, the lock slide. Then I jumped backward and cringed on the edge of the bed.

"I have a treat for you," he said when he walked in the room.

I swallowed hard. "You do?"

Daniel didn't answer for a beat, just stared at me with one of his creepily serene smiles. Finally, he reached out an arm. "Are you ready?"

My heartbeat sped up, and a tiny flash of hope licked at the bottom of my gut.

Was he letting me go?

He clamped a hand around my arm and pulled me up. I walked with him, stepping carefully, my mind reeling as he guided me down the short hallway, as he led me into the kitchen, as he pushed me down in a kitchen chair.

The table was set with candles. Actual plates, silverware. Daniel looked proud, still standing too close.

"What do you think?"

But I couldn't answer him. My eyes were locked on the television screen, on the picture flashing in front of me. A body had been found. A blond. A girl.

Everly Byer.

Daniel saw me watching. "Hope…" he started.

I took a step back. Looked around. The doors were locked. The windows, clamped shut. There was nowhere to run but back, back to the room. I didn't know what else to do so I sprinted, slamming the door hard behind me.

"Hope!" Daniel slammed a fist against the door and I crumbled, safe in my own prison.

Everly was dead. Everly was dead, and I would be too if I stayed here and let Daniel do what he wanted with me.

I was never going to let that happen. I was going to get out of there.

I paced the room, stalking. There was nothing to use as a weapon. The stuffed animals were soft and stupid, mocking me with their sewn-on smiles. I tossed them all to the ground and yanked on the shelves, throwing my entire body weight against the walls, but they must have been bolted on or something because they didn't give at all. I pulled a pillow from the case and shoved some books inside, waving the lethal pillowcase around like a mace. I tried it gently against my leg just to be sure. The soft fabric muffled the sting. I added more books. Obnoxious, but not painful. I tossed the whole thing against the one long window in the room, desperately hoping for a satisfying, freeing shatter. The pillowcase slammed against the window, books slapping out. The window bowed and clacked like thunder but didn't shatter, didn't crack. I crumbled to the floor, and Daniel was at the door.

I heard the locks slide.

One, two, three.

He pushed the door open, his eyes skittering through the room until they settled on me.

"Are you okay? Hope, Hope, are you hurt?" He took a tentative step toward me, and I cowered back, my feet kicking at the carpet, struggling for purchase.

"Stay away from me."

He paused and cocked his head, his eyes still all over me, taking me in, studying me like the caged animal I was.

"It's okay, Hope." Daniel crouched, putting the newspaper he was carrying on my desk.

"Don't touch me. Just leave me alone."

I watched Daniel swallow slowly, watched his Adam's apple bob in his throat. He looked like he wanted to say something. There was a thin, filmy mist over his eyes, and he swallowed again. I almost felt bad. Almost.

"Do you want something to eat? I cooked for you, and you ruined it."

"I don't want anything from you, Daniel. Not now and not ever." I barely spoke through clenched teeth. "Get out."

"You'll change your mind." Unfazed.

He closed the door with a soft click, and I listened to each lock slide, then counted his footsteps until they faded away. I refused to let myself feel hopeless. I refused to be helpless. I might be locked inside this horrible zoo, but I wouldn't be caged. I wouldn't languish and die here.

I snatched the newspaper Daniel left behind and got a swift punch in the gut.

The headline.

The picture.

Everly.

I chewed the inside of my cheek as I scanned the article. I went right to the second half.

Police have been close-lipped about the details of the crime, state of the body, and probable cause of death. Suffice to say that they suspect that Everly was the victim of a probable homicide.

"We will not be releasing an official statement on cause of death until the coroner has had sufficient time to complete his investigation. We will say, however, that details of how and where the body was found indicate foul play or, at the very least, suspicious circumstances. Let us continue to keep vigilant, and if anyone has any details or further information, please contact the police department's tip line."

Witnesses noted that the body was found in a shallow grave, indicating that the suspect did try to cover his tracks.

"She was slightly off the beaten path, covered with a loose shower of dirt and stacks of broken tree branches, but it was pretty obvious that the killer didn't care too much to keep her hidden. The branches came from the healthy trees right on the side of the trail and were just tossed on top of her."

Other than statements by the eyewitnesses who located the body, no one else has come forward to offer any other information. Police are asking residents to contact them if they have any information—even if it doesn't seem pertinent.

"We're talking about a strange car in the area, someone you don't recognize. Really, anything that seems or seemed out of the ordinary, even if it doesn't or didn't seem necessarily suspicious," police say.

My stomach closed in on itself.

Daniel's white truck. The scratches on his face and arms. The dirt caked underneath his fingernails.

"I had something to take care of…"

Could it have been Everly?

My heartbeat sped up. The blood pulsed against my temples, and I felt my pupils dilate and swirl. I wanted to breathe. I told myself to breathe, but my lungs had compressed, and I couldn't get a breath. I could feel the tears burning the edges of my eyes, and my whole body started to shake, ice water coursing through my veins.

I was trapped in a house with a murderer.

My eyes went to the remnants of the McDonald's, and my throat started to close. Had he poisoned me? Or was he going to kill me some other way?

No.

"You'll fall in love with me," he had said, "the way that I love you…" He loved me. He wasn't going to hurt me. But Everly…

A shallow grave…loosely covered…branches, dirt…

The scratches on his forearms, on his face. Everly had fought. She had tried to fight for her life. She had lost.

I thought of those same arms around me. The sinewy muscle of Daniel's forearm as he clamped it over my chest, as he used it to pin my arms to my sides. The pinprick, the insulin.

Everly had tried to fight. She had fought for her life—and lost.

I ripped Everly's picture from the paper and studied it, willing my heart to beat at a normal level, willing myself to breathe slowly but surely, in and out.

I would fight.

I would kill Daniel if I had to.

I was going to fight for my life, and I wouldn't lose.

FIFTY-ONE

Tony

Bellingham said they would come with a warrant, that it was just a matter of time.

I didn't have time, and neither did Hope.

"I can't just sit around and do nothing." I was at home, sitting at our dining room table with both of my parents, Alice, and Bellingham. We were eating fast food with the curtains drawn. The kitchen garbage was already overflowing with take-out wrappers and pizza boxes because there was a swarm of reporters out front again. Ever since I'd refused the search, they had become rampant, crazy, like a mass of barking dogs. It was hard to believe that was only a few hours ago.

"You're doing exactly what you need to be doing, Tony," Bellingham said.

I poked at a cold fry and stared at it. "I don't feel like anyone is doing anything worthwhile."

My mother put her hand on my arm and squeezed gently. "Everyone is working to find Hope, Tony."

"Are they?" I didn't mean it to sound sharp, but it did. "I feel like all anyone is working to do is to throw me in jail." Bellingham, my mother, and my father were all staring at me. I didn't care until I saw that Alice was too, her chin slightly dropped, cute kid rosebud lips a perfect O in a face that didn't understand.

"Is Tony going to go to jail, Mama?" The tremor in her voice ripped me apart as my mother and father jumped in to console her. I left the table, hearing them reassure Alice, telling her I wasn't going anywhere, but I wondered how they could be so sure. No one cared about finding Hope anymore.

No one cared but me.

I must have dozed when I went back to my room because when I woke up, the lights were blazing but it was pitch-black out my bedroom window. I paused for a second, sucking in my breath, wondering if Everly would appear again, would start knocking.

Then it hit me that she was dead.

FIFTY-TWO

Hope

There was no clock in here. There was no way to mark the time other than sun up versus sun down. I thought about stupid old-timey prison movies where the hero was stuck in some godforsaken cell scratching out the days with hash marks on a wall. I considered doing that, but all at once I refused. I wouldn't be here long enough.

I think it was nearly morning now. I only knew that because the light that filtered in through the thick-as-a-wall plastic window was gray and cold-looking, and I could hear Daniel in the kitchen and vaguely smell bacon and eggs frying. It turned my stomach and made me hungry all at once. I wanted to eat—God, I wanted to eat—but that would mean Daniel would have to come back to this room, come back to me.

And then he knocked on the door.

The fact that he knocked made me livid and terrified at the same time. I couldn't get out. He was the only one who could come in. And yet he knocked, like this was all perfectly normal, and I was some houseguest who could come and go as I pleased, who wanted to be here at all.

He knocked again.

"Yeah?"

He cleared his throat. "Breakfast is ready."

I heard him start on the locks: one, two, three. I felt my eyes widen, felt the adrenaline crashing through my veins. The door opened and he stood there, looking every inch a man, nothing like the monster I'd built up in my mind.

"I'm not hungry," I spat out, hating myself for the way I stepped back for each of his steps forward.

He didn't break his stride or his smile. "You need to eat."

I shook my head; that was all I could muster.

"Come on, Hope."

He was on me, and I crumbled in the corner, tucked in the sliver of space between the desk and the wall. "Get away from me."

Daniel sighed. "We're going to be friends. You'll see." He smiled a little bigger, a little harder. "We're going to be more than friends."

"I'll never be anything to you. You'll never be anything to me but some kidnapping freak motherfucker."

The smile dropped from Daniel's lips. "That's not a very nice thing to say. Especially after everything I've done for you."

I wanted to explode, but the fight left me. "Just leave me alone."

"No, you're going to eat. We're going to have a meal like two civilized people."

He came for me, and I spat, my teeth gnashing out at the arm he offered. I tasted flesh, blood. I savored the sound of Daniel's yelp—pained, surprised, outraged. He slapped me across the face, hard. I could feel my teeth rattle, but I kept them sunk into Daniel's meaty flesh. I could feel his blood mixing with my saliva, the molten concoction dribbling over my chin.

He hit me again and again, and finally I let go, spitting a mouthful of blood onto the carpet and glaring at him, daring him to hit me again. I was a wild animal. I would tear him limb from limb with my teeth if I had to. I didn't know how or when it happened, but I was crouching now, hands and bare feet digging into the carpet, ready to spring. He held my stare.

"Be a good girl, Hope."

I pounced. Pummeled him. Head to chest. I bashed my forehead hard against his collarbone, scratched and clawed and bit at whatever I made contact with. My hands were around his throat. I was squeezing. He gurgled and groaned, and some sad, strangled wet breath came from his chest. He was pushing at me, hitting, kicking.

His knee made contact with my rib cage, and my mouth exploded open, a deep, loud *oof* coming out.

I squeezed tighter at his throat, pinching bits of skin between my fingertips and digging my nails in.

I knew I was being hit, kicked, but the pain didn't register. I wouldn't let it register. Daniel shoved me hard, and I had to loosen my grip. I heard the sound of flesh against bone, the crack of bone against bone, but the pain didn't hit me for a full minute after.

My head was spinning, my eyes wobbling in my own head, and Daniel was painted in swirls of black. I was falling backward, losing consciousness.

And then I saw it again.

The edge of the forgotten newspaper.

Everly Byer. Dead.

Daniel.

I gritted teeth that felt loose and paper-thin. I expected them to crack, but they didn't, and every muscle in my body was bolstered by this fact. I went for Daniel again.

I felt his fingers on my flesh, pulling at my shirt.

The rage was overtaken by fear.

Don't, don't, don't—

But he didn't.

I felt the prongs against my skin first. Icy cold metal. In a millisecond, I was on fire. My skin felt too tight. My bones protruded. My teeth rattled, and the electricity blossomed from my rib cage, from the tiny points of those two cold prongs and up and down my spine. My head wobbled like a cheap toy at the end of my spine. My toes spread, my hands fisted, and I was sweating everywhere. I blinked it into my eyes, tasted it as it rolled over my lips, felt the rivulets between my breasts, down the center of my back, pouring from my underarms.

The current stopped, and I flopped to the ground, my body molten, my mouth hanging slack because I couldn't work my muscles. My brain couldn't fire off a single command. I caught my breath as Daniel hung over me, staring. He slowly moved a hand in front of my face, close enough for my eyes to focus on the hot-pink thing he had in his hands.

It looked like a ladies' electric razor.

He smiled, another of those hideous, slick, twisted grins, and I watched his thumb move to the side of the little pink machine, watched as he depressed a black button.

Electricity.

The cracking, horrible sound: half-harnessed electricity, half memory of bones clacking against each other. My body involuntarily stiffened, my eyes glued to the volts of blue light pulsing between the two tiny tongs.

Daniel flicked the stun gun off. "It belonged to your friend Everly."

I looked up, tried to focus.

"Why her? She was a phony, Hope. She was trying to take your place. I knew it would make you happy to have her gone. I did good, right?"

FIFTY-THREE

Tony

Once again, Bellingham told me to sit tight. To wait for his cue. I didn't. I had started this whole thing, even if Hope had kept it rolling, and I was going to end it. I slammed my car door and drove to the police station, every mile closer, my throat tightening, my heartbeat speeding up.

MacNamara was at front desk when I walked into the station.

"Tony," she said, eyebrows up. She looked surprised to see me.

"I want to make a statement."

She looked over my shoulder. "Shouldn't we wait for your attorney?"

I shook my head. "I need to do this now."

"Okay, but we need to get your parents or guardians—"

"The reason why I was the last person to talk to Hope Jensen is because she was getting me back for putting all of her personal information online. I shared her location, and she wanted to get me back, so she staged a kidnapping."

MacNamara just blinked at me.

"Tony?"

Pace walked into the precinct with the chief of police on his tail. Right behind him in a flurry of camera flashes and boom lights were Bruce and Becky Jensen, looking television perfect.

"What's going on here?" the chief wanted to know.

MacNamara stood up and came to my side. "Tony Gardner wants to make a statement. Mr. and Mrs. Jensen, if you would like to come with me—"

"No." I had no idea where my confidence came from, but I didn't question it. "They need to hear this. Hope is in trouble. She wasn't, but she is now. She staged a kidnapping. She—"

"We were just about to host a press conference," Bruce Jensen said briskly.

"This is what the press needs to know. That Hope is out there, and she's in trouble. It was my fault. I put her information online, and Hope wanted to teach me a lesson. She pretended she was being kidnapped. She wanted me to believe that someone actually took her, and now I think that someone actually did."

I waited for Bruce and Becky to spring into action. For police lights to start flashing, for something to start happening, but nothing did.

"Are you hearing me? Hope is really in trouble." It felt like the world dropped into molasses slow motion, and then I understood. Hope wasn't just in on the prank. Her parents were too.

FIFTY-FOUR

Hope

It took everything I had to stay composed. "You did really good, Daniel." I bit the words hard. "Thank you for everything."

He beamed. "You're welcome."

"So you watched me so that you could find me."

Daniel pumped his head. "I was going to rescue you, but you came to me. That made me very happy."

"Now we can start our life together."

"I've been waiting so long to hear you say that."

I nodded carefully, then glanced around. "I think we need a fresh start, don't you? A new place. Something that's…us."

"I couldn't agree with you more."

FIFTY-FIVE

Tony

Knowing hit me square in the chest, the realization so horrifyingly overwhelming that I gasped audibly.

"Oh my God. You knew about this. You knew."

The Jensens shared an uncomfortable look—fleeting, miniscule—immediately replaced by practiced professionalism. "I don't know what you are trying to imply, Mr. Gardner—"

"I'm not implying it," I said, bolder now. "I'm saying it. You knew what Hope was planning, and you…you staged the thing yourself."

Bruce's eyes went steel-blade cold. "You better check yourself."

"Your daughter is in trouble. This is not some publicity stunt. It went *sideways*, Mr. Jensen. It went wrong."

"Can someone get this kid out of here?" Becky had her hands on her hips, then seemed to remember that she was playing the part of the tortured mother. "I can't deal with this, with our baby, Hope, missing…and now…and now…" She fanned herself, the act so dramatic it was almost comical.

"What exactly are you saying, Tony?" Pace asked.

I sidestepped Pace and went straight for Bruce Jensen. "You knew what Hope was planning, didn't you?"

Bruce looked hard at me and avoided Pace and MacNamara. "You don't want to do this, Tony. Just play along, okay?"

"Are you kidding me?"

Becky made a beeline toward me, her voice a slight octave above a whisper. "Hope had a plan. We overheard it. She was going out with her friend. No harm, no foul. Just play along for the cameras, okay?"

Bruce and Becky were framed in the harsh fluorescent lights, and I saw them then for everything that Hope said that they were: Desperate. Fame hungry. So rolled up in their own agenda they had no idea Hope's high school revenge plan had taken on a life of its own. That their own daughter was in danger while they rolled film. For the first time in a long time, I felt truly sorry for Hope.

FIFTY-SIX

Hope

Daniel had the stun gun in his pocket. He had a knife in the kitchen and a gun somewhere in his house. I had nothing, but I would get out of here. I would get free.

"So you know I'm a good guy. I'm saving you. I saved you."

I could see that Daniel really believed what he was saying so I nodded. "Yes, I see that now."

He beamed. "I'm going to cook us dinner. And I'm going to start preparing now."

I cleared my throat. "Can I come in the kitchen with you? I think I"—I almost choked on the words—"I think I would like to be with you right now. I don't want to be alone."

A crimson wash went over Daniel's cheeks. "That would be nice."

"You'll have to unlock me."

"Okay."

I stood a little too quickly, and he narrowed his eyes. "You're tricky, but I have this." He brandished the stun gun, and an involuntary sweat broke out all over my body. He pushed the thing against my skin and I bristled, every muscle tightening, teeth clenched, but nothing happened.

"*Zzzz!*" he said. "I wasn't going to do it, but if you try anything…" He pulled the machine from my skin and flicked the button, the blue-white electricity crackling to life. "Okay?"

I nodded, silent, terrified, but still determined.

Daniel went to work unlocking the clamp around my ankle with one hand, the stun gun at the ready in the other. I made a show of being a good girl, of not moving. I even forced a sweet smile and tried to make small talk. "The room looks nice. Thank you for cooking dinner."

He shuffled me down the hall in that same slow walk I was beginning to get used to and despise, and when we entered the living room, the television was on again. This time was the news, and once again it was my parents. Daniel turned the volume off before I heard them speak.

"They're getting really famous," he said again. He pulled out a chair. "You can sit right here."

I sat dutifully, and Daniel rifled through a drawer and produced two zip ties. I shook my head sternly. "You don't have to," I said simply.

"I think I do."

"I heard what you said. You're a good guy. Just saving me from my parents."

I could almost see the cogs turning in Daniel's head. He wanted to believe me, looked like he was desperate to. I leaned forward, let my hand find his, even as his touch made my skin crawl. "I understand now."

"You do?"

I nodded.

"I'll sit here, and next time, I can cook you dinner."

Daniel pumped his head. I clasped my hands in my lap, and plastered on my sweetest, more serene smile. I stayed silent and unmoving while he pulled things out of the cabinets, the refrigerator, even though each move made me want to flinch, made my muscles remember the shock of electricity and recoil.

"We're going to be happy, Hope. You and me."

FIFTY-SEVEN

Tony

"I'm not going to play along. The person who has Hope isn't playing along."

Becky's grip was firm on my arm. "His name is Rustin. He's a friend."

"That's what I've been trying to tell you. She's not with Rustin anymore. She's gone."

Becky blinked. Bruce blanched.

The red lights of the cameras clicked on. Light flooded the station. For once, Bruce and Becky Jensen were caught off guard, caught looking slightly imperfect.

"Don't film this," Becky said.

"We're not rolling yet," Bruce barked.

Pace stepped forward and addressed the Jensens. "Where is Hope?"

"We're going live in five, four…" the cameraman started.

"This isn't about fame anymore. This is about your daughter!"

"Three, two—"

"Where is she?"

FIFTY-EIGHT

Hope

I squinted at the screen. "What's going on?"

The news on the television broke into a disheveled scene at the police department. My parents looked awkward, pained. There were police officers and—Tony? I rushed to turn up the volume, but Daniel snatched me by the arm.

"You said you wouldn't!"

I twisted the volume knob just in time to hear Tony, to see my parents pale.

"See? See, Hope? They don't love you."

It was all a farce. A ruse. Like everything else in my life, like the fake room in Daniel's house.

I saw the edge of frying pan Daniel had set on the stove. I lunged.

It made a satisfying *thwap* when it made contact with the side of Daniel's head. He doubled over, crumbled in front of me, the Atlas Security patch glaring up at me. He wouldn't have known me if my parents hadn't dedicated my whole life to their viewing audience.

He wouldn't have found me if I hadn't needed to get the last laugh. With a shaking hand, I went for his pocket. Slid out his cell phone. Dialed the number of the one person in my life who believed in me. Who saw me.

Who I had sold out.

"Tony…" My voice was a cracked whisper.

EPILOGUE

Tony

The story of Bruce, Becky, and Hope was all over the news again, on every channel. I was a footnote, the poor sap who got dragged into the whole situation. Hope was famous. Bruce and Becky were infamous. Hope didn't even come to school anymore; she was too busy giving interviews, playing the doe-eyed ingénue whose whole life was manipulated by her parents' unquenchable thirst for the spotlight.

My parents, Alice, and I were sitting on our couch when another one of Hope's interviews came on television. I moved to change the channel but my mother stopped me. "Let's hear what she has to say."

The interviewer asked the usual questions: how Hope was coping, what life was like after captivity, if she still spoke to "the boy" who made her parents come clean on national television. Hope answered expertly, and even I was convinced. Then she was asked, "Hope, do you blame your parents for manipulating your kidnapping?"

Hope blinked, blue eyes wide. "You know, Alan, I don't. I'm just not the kind of girl who believes in getting revenge."

ACKNOWLEDGMENTS

All books are a labor of love but this one included physical labor as well—fifteen and a half hours of it! Thank you so much to Sourcebooks superstar editors Annette Pollert-Morgan and Annie Berger for being so flexible when my daughter decided to usurp my book due date with her birth date. Thank you also to amazing agent Amberly Finarelli for hours of book and baby counsel. Huge thanks to the "Le Boo Crew": Julie, Joni, Rich, Debbie, and Christina for the hugs, critiques, and "butt in chair, hands on keys" commands. And, above all, thank you to all my fans who continue to read, write, and inspire me every day.

ABOUT THE AUTHOR

Hannah Jayne decided to be an author in the second grade. She couldn't spell and had terrible ideas, but she kept at it, and many (many) years and nearly twenty books later, she gets to live her dream and mainly does it in her pajamas.

She lives with her rock-star husband, their new baby, and their three overweight cats in the San Francisco Bay Area, and is always on the lookout for a good mystery, a good story, or a great adventure.